Praise fc

"Fresh and exciting, humorous and action-packed...urban fantasy at its best."

–Ilona Andrews, #1 New York Times *bestselling author of the Kate Daniels series*

"Makenna Fraser brings Southern sass, smarts, and charm to the mean streets of Manhattan as she battles monsters and other magical beings."

–Jennifer Estep, New York Times *bestselling author of the Elemental Assassin novels*

"Plenty more gasp- and laughter-inducing adventures...this is a thrilling series, so hang on tight, for things are going to get seriously bumpy!"

–RT Book Reviews

"A word of warning, don't start this book unless you have a solid block set aside as you simply will not be able to put it down."

–A Book Obsession

"Shearin has been on my auto-buy list for years. She is able to combine humor, mystery, suspense, slow-burn romance, high stakes, and her own spin on the supernatural into a cohesive whole. I'm addicted to finding out what will happen next in the SPI Files."

–Bookpushers

"There is so much action that you can't put this book down...fun and truly great adventure stories."

–Night Owl Romance

"There are twists, turns, danger, romance, action, but more importantly—lots of fun... Laugh out loud funny... A brilliantly addictive urban fantasy s

ır Tree

D1616886

Praise for the Raine Benares Novels

ALL SPELL BREAKS LOOSE

"Exceptional…Shearin has proven herself to be an expert storyteller with the enviable ability to provide both humor and jaw-dropping action."

—RT Book Reviews

"*All Spell Breaks Loose* not only lived up to my expectations but was even BETTER!"

—Dangerous Romance

CON & CONJURE

"Tons of action and adventure but it also has a bit of romance and humor…All of the characters are excellent…The complexities of the world that Ms. Shearin has developed are fabulous."

—Night Owl Reviews

"Action packed and fast paced, this was a fabulous read."

—Fresh Fiction

"*Con & Conjure* is a great addition to a wonderful series, and I'm looking forward to *All Spell Breaks Loose* and whatever else [Shearin writes] with high anticipation."

—Dear Author

BEWITCHED & BETRAYED

"Once again, Ms. Shearin has given her readers a book that you don't want to put down. With Raine, the adventures never end."

—Night Owl Reviews

"*Bewitched & Betrayed* might just be the best in the series so far!… an amazingly exciting fourth installment that really tugs at the heart strings."

—Ink and Paper

"If you're new to Shearin's work, and you enjoy fantasy interspersed with an enticing romance, a little bit of humor, and a whole lot of grade-A action, this is the series for you."

–Lurv a la Mode

THE TROUBLE WITH DEMONS

"The book reads more like an urban fantasy with pirates and sharp wit and humor. I found the mix quite refreshing. Lisa Shearin's fun, action-packed writing style gives this world life and vibrancy."

–Fresh Fiction

"Lisa Shearin represents that much needed voice in fantasy that combines practiced craft and a wicked sense of humor."

–Bitten by Books

"The brisk pace and increasingly complex character development propel the story on a rollercoaster ride through demons, goblins, elves, and mages while maintaining a satisfying level of romantic attention…that will leave readers chomping at the bit for more."

–Monsters and Critics

"This book has the action starting as soon as you start the story and it keeps going right to the end…All of the characters are interesting, from the naked demon queen to the Guardians guarding Raine. All have a purpose and it comes across with clarity and detail."

–Night Owl Reviews

ARMED & MAGICAL

"Fresh, original, and fall-out-of-your-chair funny, Lisa Shearin's *Armed & Magical* combines deft characterization, snarky dialogue, and nonstop action—plus a yummy hint of romance—to create one of the best reads of the year. This book is a bona fide winner, the series a keeper, and Shearin a definite star on the rise."

–Linnea Sinclair, RITA Award-winning author of Rebels and Lovers

"An exciting, catch-me-if-you-can, lightning-fast-paced tale of magic and evil filled with goblins, elves, mages, and a hint of love interest that will leave fantasy readers anxiously awaiting Raine's next adventure."

–Monsters and Critics

"The kind of book you hope to find when you go to the bookstore. It takes you away to a world of danger, magic, and adventure, and it does so with dazzling wit and clever humor. It's gritty, funny, and sexy—a wonderful addition to the urban fantasy genre. I absolutely loved it. From now on Lisa Shearin is on my auto-buy list!"

–Ilona Andrews, #1 New York Times *bestselling author of* Magic Shifts

"*Armed & Magical*, like its predecessor, is an enchanting read from the very first page. I absolutely loved it. Shearin weaves a web of magic with a dash of romance that thoroughly snares the reader. She's definitely an author to watch!"

–Anya Bast, New York Times *bestselling author of* Embrace of the Damned

MAGIC LOST, TROUBLE FOUND

"Take a witty, kick-ass heroine and put her in a vividly realized fantasy world where the stakes are high, and you've got a fun, page-turning read in Magic Lost, Trouble Found. I can't wait to read more of Raine Benares's adventures."

–Shanna Swendson, author of Don't Hex with Texas

"A wonderful fantasy tale full of different races and myths and legends [that] are drawn so perfectly readers will believe they actually exist. Raine is a strong female, a leader who wants to do the right thing even when she isn't sure what that is…Lisa Shearin has the magic touch."

–Midwest Book Review

This book is a work of fiction. The characters, incidents, and dialogue are drawn from the author's imagination and are not to be construed as real. Any resemblance to actual events or persons, living or dead, is entirely coincidental.

THE PHOENIX ILLUSION © 2018 by Lisa Shearin
Published by Murwood Media, LLC

Editor: Betsy Mitchell
Copyeditor: Martha Trachtenberg
Cover artist: Julie Dillon
Book designer: Angie Hodapp

ISBN 978-1-7327226-0-6

THE PHOENIX ILLUSION

A SPI FILES NOVEL

LISA SHEARIN

1

It was the third night in a row of strobe-like lightning with no thunder and no rain. That should have tipped me off— it should have tipped us all off—but it didn't.

I'd been having too much fun lately. Not that I didn't deserve it. I did. Deserved it, needed it, wanted it, and welcomed it and its bearer with open arms. Besides, it was my birthday. Who didn't deserve to have fun on their birthday?

We were down the street from SPI headquarters at the Full Moon. The neighborhood bar and grill was our favorite hangout, so I'd picked it for my party.

Note that I said "party," not "surprise party."

I hate surprises. As a kid, it didn't matter how good my family thought they were at hiding surprises from me, I knew one was coming and I didn't like it. Even if a person I trusted told me I'd love it.

I might like—or even love—what the surprise *was,* but I hated what it *did.* To me.

I was one of those people who got a side order of anxiety to go with any kind of surprise.

Maybe it all went back to me being a control freak—and a terrible liar.

What if I got a present and I didn't like it? When I was little, I had an aunt who made dresses for me. Let's just say she had a thing for pink bows—a *lot* of pink bows. Big ones. It almost made me want to stop having birthday parties. Nothing was worse than unwrapping a present and not being able to fake a thrilled response. I didn't want to hurt anyone's feelings. It wasn't that I didn't like getting presents. I did. It was simply better for everyone concerned that I knew what it was beforehand.

My name is Makenna Fraser and I work for SPI (Supernatural Protection and Investigations). In my professional life, I have a skill that eliminates a certain kind of surprise. I'm a seer. I can see through any shield, ward, or spell a supernatural being can use to disguise itself from the human population. My ability also applies to cloaks and veils that render their wearers invisible. SPI is in the supernatural criminal apprehension business. You can't apprehend what you can't see. That's where I come in. I go with our agents or commando teams and point out the supernatural perps they can't see, so they can take them down or out.

That wasn't to say my professional life wasn't chock-full of surprises. It was. The kind only someone named Rambo would enjoy, but at least I didn't have to act happy to see them. In fact, most times it was perfectly acceptable for me to shoot it full of lead or—on occasion—silver. Or better yet, get out of the way so our commandos could do the same. As much as I wanted to be as badass as my coworkers, I'd come to accept that it simply wasn't gonna happen, but that didn't stop me from training and trying. It was the least I could do for the people who had to work with me.

I was from the mountains of North Carolina, a proud Southern girl, and was determined to stay that way, even though I now worked and lived in New York. I loved my adopted home and would—and had—put my life on the line to defend it and its people, but I'd always consider Weird Sisters, North Carolina, home.

Today in the office, I'd gotten a cake in the break room, and been on the receiving end of an embarrassing (to everyone concerned) rendition of "Happy Birthday." The party at the Full Moon was a casual gathering of my closest friends/coworkers, with dinner and open bar. The owners were like a work mom and dad to us all, and they'd offered to close the bar for the night for us—and for them.

It was the week before a full moon outside the Full Moon.

The owners were werewolves.

Bill and Nancy Garrison were from my home state of North Carolina and offered a slice of Southern hospitality to New Yorkers. The Garrisons had embraced the hide-in-plain-sight credo of supernatural concealment. They billed the Full Moon as New York's Official Werewolf Bar and had decorated it accordingly. Heck, there was even a little gift shop up front. It was a meat lover's paradise where the steaks were rare, the barbecue tangy, and the iced tea had enough sugar in it to make a spoon stand on end. It also had the distinction of having one of the best collections of single malt scotches in the city, scotches that'd put even more hair on a werewolf's chest.

The coming of the monthly full moon made life awkward for the Garrisons and two of their staff who'd come with them from south of the Mason-Dixon line—their office manager and the head bartender. The rest of their employees were either supernatural beings or what SPI called clued-in humans (those who wouldn't scream and run away at the sight of a furry and fanged boss).

Going all furry and fierce once a month made it somewhat difficult to run a business, especially a restaurant. As the Full Moon's barbecue pit master, Bill's monthly inconvenience of increased hairiness presented a big problem with potential health code violations, not to mention the possibility of scorched fur. In another couple of days, Bill would hand the cooking honors over to his assistant and the human chef who ruled the roost in the kitchen.

It's a misconception that werewolves go stark raving loony during the full moon. They're more irritable during their special time of the month, but they aren't gonna go nuts and rip your throat out. Unless you give them a good reason, in which case, they'd be glad to oblige you.

All of those in attendance were friends of mine who were also coworkers or people connected to work who knew what we did. My partner Ian and his girlfriend Kylie were here. Ian Byrne was SPI's top agent, and Kylie O'Hara was the director of SPI's Media Relations department. She lived for crisis management, and when you were an agency responsible for hiding the supernatural world from humans, you pretty much lived in crisis mode. To add an extra touch of irony, Kylie wasn't human. She was a dryad. Ian was human. Mostly. Way back in his ancestry was an ancient Irish demigod, but he didn't let that get in the way of being one of the guys.

SPI, even more than the mortal world's alphabet agencies, did work that you simply couldn't talk about. Secrets must be kept for the safety of those concerned and for ongoing investigations. SPI was the same with one big difference— even if we could talk about what we saw at work, people would think we were nuts.

SPI's best allies were humans who were in on our world's big secret and didn't freak out. Monsters were real, supernatural beings existed alongside us, and magic was as much a fact as gravity. I was sure there were people who denied the existence of gravity, just like there were those who denied other scientifically and historically proven facts and events. Some people wouldn't recognize the truth if it bit 'em and had 'em for breakfast.

There was a whole world out there that humans didn't see. Their next-door neighbors might be plain vanilla human, or they could be any number of supernatural beings with their more alarming physical features either disguised by magical spells, or with devices developed and worn for the purpose of keeping a supernatural from being identified as such by their kept-clueless neighbors and coworkers. Humans had an unfortunate tendency to go all torchy and pitchforky when they discovered inhumans anywhere in their immediate vicinity.

That was SPI's main mission: Keep the peace by keepin' 'em clueless.

My hometown was full of all kinds of supernaturals. And being a seer, I'd grown up seeing each and every one of them. For me, supernaturals were the norm rather than the exception, which was probably why I didn't think twice about having a goblin as a boyfriend.

My momma had warned me about bad boys.

Rake Danescu was a very bad boy—in all the very best ways.

Though to hear my family talk, my dad had been a bad boy. Like mother, like daughter? Moth to flame, and all that?

Rake Danescu had gone from being an SPI person of interest to being an agency ally. He was now *my* person of interest and occupied the one and only spot on my most-wanted list.

For the first time ever, I had myself a serious boyfriend. Though Rake was definitely a man, not a boy, but I had no problem with the semantics. Regardless of what the rest of the world wanted to call our relationship, it didn't change what it was.

He was mine, and I was his, and that arrangement suited me just fine.

We were supposed to have taken a trip to North Carolina so Rake could meet my family, but work had gotten in the way. Most notably, Rake's new job. He'd recently been appointed governor of the goblin colony here on Earth. It wasn't a job he wanted, but with the corruptness of the previous governor and his henchmen, Rake knew he was needed. He cared about his people and took his new responsibility very seriously. We'd postponed the trip until the end of next month.

Rake enjoyed being with my coworkers more than he did the upper-crusters at the events and parties he was expected to attend as one of New York's wealthiest men—and as the new goblin colonial governor.

He'd told me more than once that me being by his side was the only thing that made those events bearable.

To tell you the truth, "uncomfortable" was the nicest way I could describe accompanying Rake to the goblin events. A more accurate description would be "mouse in a room full of sadistic cats." Not that they necessarily wished me harm—at least not most of them—but I was a human. Goblins considered humans, as well as elves and every other supernatural race and species, to be far beneath them.

Goblins were what my Grandma Fraser would call snooty.

I think that was why Rake preferred my friends to his acquaintances. They knew who he was (a goblin spymaster), what he was (a badass dark mage), and how he was (inscrutable as all get-out), and they accepted all of it. At least they did now. That hadn't always been the case.

Rake had come a long way in their estimation.

A lot of that had to do with him putting himself in the worst kind of danger to save them from the worst kind of death. He'd been right there on the front lines with them more than once. That kind of bravery and selflessness was remembered, appreciated, and rewarded with friendship. I knew that Rake appreciated it. In his line of work, there weren't many people he could trust. As a result, Rake didn't have that many friends, and even though he hadn't come right out and said it, I could tell he was truly happy when he was around mine. Slowly but surely those defensive walls of his were coming down.

Rake walked the talk and put his money where his mouth was, and all that. As a result, folks at SPI finally believed that he didn't have an ulterior motive for any of it.

Acceptance and trust of Rake was a relatively new thing for me, too.

The night I'd met Rake had been my first day working for SPI. To get his way, Rake had never been opposed to throwing in a little seduction. Not that he wasn't good at it. He was. Oh boy, was he ever. But I'd been warned about him, and my guard had been up. Mostly. Hey, I was only human, as most goblins were all too fond of reminding me.

Maybe that was part of what had attracted Rake to me. Goblins played games. Heck, their games played games. With goblins you never knew what was real and what was just another way to get what they wanted.

They were kind of like cats in that respect. I'd always been more of a dog person, but I had a soft spot for any cat that rubbed up against me. Rake had rubbed up against me. Mostly metaphorically, but on occasion literally. I'd finally come to believe that it was because he liked me, not because he wanted anything. Well, aside from the obvious. And I had to admit, all that rubbing felt oh so much better now without any clothes in the way.

"What are you thinking?" Rake purred against my ear.

We were snuggled in a booth watching our friends getting seriously competitive at an after-dinner game of darts. Rake was politely sitting this one out because he was entirely too good at throwing sharp, stabby things. Actually, so were my coworkers. The target's bull's-eye was getting a serious workout. Bill and Nancy were gonna have to replace the board after tonight.

"Nothing," I told him. It was the go-to answer when you got caught thinking something you didn't want to admit—at least not in public, surrounded by your coworkers.

"You were smiling." Now so was he.

Two could play that game. "Hmm, was I? I can't imagine why."

"Now you're blushing."

"Must be warm in here."

Rake scooched even closer. "Could it be something else?"

I made a show of pondering. "Um…no."

"Well, if you're sure." His fangs darted in for a quick nip on my ear.

He knew that made me crazy. But I knew what made him even crazier. Payback would be sweet. Later.

Suddenly, a tingle that had nothing to do with Rake's nibbling ran down my back.

Rake had frozen, all his senses on high alert.

In seconds, the pressure in the room increased to an excruciating level and immediately dropped. It was like the onset of the worst sinus headache ever. Then my ears popped. Painfully.

Kenji Hayashi, half-elf and SPI's IT and communications guru, quickly stuffed a napkin under his now bleeding nose. He wasn't the only one.

The pressure drop was followed by a boom from outside. Close-by outside.

It wasn't an explosion, at least not the kind caused by explosives. It was magic. The big kind. The kind that didn't happen by accident.

Then the power went out.

The bar area of the Full Moon was away from the restaurant's front windows. It was so dark back here that I couldn't see my hand in front of my face. The Garrisons had emergency lights, but apparently those weren't working, either.

I felt and heard Rake quickly slide out of the booth. "Everyone stay put." His voice came from halfway to the front doors. "I'll take a look." As a goblin, Rake had some serious night vision.

The Full Moon was warded. The Garrisons didn't have defensive magic of their own, and most times they didn't need it. Most times fur, fangs, and fury were all that were needed to deal with any incident.

This wasn't one of those times.

We considered the Full Moon as an extension of SPI HQ. As such, the Garrisons had allowed our battlemages to ward the bar with enough defensive magic to keep out anything SPI's enemies could conjure up.

And while the Garrisons didn't have any magical skills, they had an ability the rest of us didn't. A highly developed sense of smell.

Rummaging sounds came from the bar. Seconds later, two battery-powered lanterns were switched on. Nancy brought one over to the seating area. Then she paused and sniffed the air. "Fire."

Bill raised his nose that in a few days would be a muzzle and took a whiff. "Half a block east."

A fun night with friends had officially turned into unwanted business.

Training and instinct took over. We weren't the NYPD, so we couldn't storm out the front doors with our guns drawn. Not to mention storming anywhere would've been stupid until we knew what we were dealing with. But now that we had light, we could go find out.

A second boom shook the floor under our feet. Rake was

standing on the sidewalk outside the front doors. He was staring down the street in shock. Ian, Kylie, and I joined him.

Adrenaline was good for all kinds of things. It gave you time to figure out how not to die a horrible and messy death. It also gave you time to figure out just what the heck you were looking at, and how best to deal with it without dying said horrible and messy death. That being said, adrenaline was absolutely no help when it came to telling my mind what to do with what I was seeing.

It was that bizarre.

There was a vacant lot two buildings down from where we stood on the sidewalk—a lot that had been vacant when we'd walked to the Full Moon from work.

It wasn't vacant anymore.

A three-story building was smack dab in the middle of it and was fully engulfed. Sirens in the distance signaled that New York's finest firefighters were on the way. The nearest station was only six blocks away, and I was no fire expert, but even I knew there wasn't going to be anything left to save. The fire was burning too hot.

Too hot for a normal fire.

But the air wasn't hot. It was downright cold. Cold enough to see my breath. The temperature had to have dropped at least forty degrees from the time we'd walked over from headquarters. The flames engulfing the structure were circling in on themselves toward the center of the structure like a tornado; and above the fire the sky glowed like a golden aurora borealis.

The fire and the glowing sky were the only light in the immediate area.

None of this was normal.

Rake stared in shock and disbelief. "That's my house," he managed.

I heard him, but that couldn't have been what he said. "Your *what*?"

"My house. From Regor."

2

Working for SPI, you saw some strange…stuff. This took the cake—and any ice cream that came with it.

Regor was the goblin capital.

On Rake's home world.

Those of us who'd heard Rake say what the building was and where it'd come from were wearing variations of his disbelieving stare. I started to cough at the smoke in the air. Apparently, I'd also had my mouth hanging open.

Rake's dark eyes were intent and moving rapidly over the structure. I felt his magic reaching out, toward the engulfed house, scanning the interior…

There was a stab of panic in my gut. "Is anyone—"

"No." He listened and hesitated. "No. There's no one. It was being renovated. My parents are living at our country house."

Thank God.

Kenji had his phone out. Weirdness at this level needed to be called in, especially when said weirdness was happening mere blocks from our worldwide headquarters.

Kenji poked at his phone's screen and swore. "Does anyone's phone work?"

Mine was in my purse, and I'd left that in the booth. Several of my coworkers had theirs in various pockets. All the screens were dark.

Dead phones, no electricity, a funky glow in the sky, and a house from another world on fire.

"Cendi, can you get through?" Kylie asked.

Cendi Tremont was a seriously gifted telepath. She could she talk mind-to-mind to anyone in a fifty-mile radius. For SPI agents, if she knew you were in a meeting, she could telepathically send a text to your phone. And she was an absolute blast on our SPI girls' nights out.

Cendi stepped back into Full Moon's doorway, bowed her head, and stood motionless for a few moments. She glanced back at us and gave a thumbs-up.

At least something was working.

"Who?" Kylie asked.

"Ms. Sagadraco and Mr. Moreau," Cendi said.

SPI's boss lady herself and her right-hand man now knew what was happening. Cendi didn't play around.

"I also own the empty lot," Rake told us.

Ian swore, Kylie added to it, and I couldn't have agreed more with their word choices.

A very large and public situation had just turned from a literal and metaphorical three-alarm fire into an impending catastrophe.

Rake's house from Rake's world burning on Rake's lot. Accident? Random celestial convergence? Nope and nope.

The firemen and police might not know this wasn't an accident, at least not yet, but we did.

And they would. Soon.

New York's law enforcement community frowned on arson, regardless of the cause. We didn't have much time before someone official started asking unanswerable questions.

Like why there was a building burning on a vacant lot.

The firefighters had responded to a report of a building on fire. They came, they saw a building burning. Their job was to make the building not burn anymore, not ask who put a building on a lot that had been vacant hours, or maybe minutes, before. They had one job—at least for now—and they were doing it.

When the fire was out and cooled enough to get in there, they were gonna have a lot of questions.

Police were moving onlookers closest to the blaze to a safe distance. There was an outer perimeter where a couple hundred people were straining to get a look at what would have been trending on local Twitter feeds by now, that is if anyone's phones had been working. I scanned the crowd and was glad to see a lot of disappointed tweeters. At least something good was coming from the power outage.

Nothing brought out rubberneckers like traffic accidents and fires. Used to be, folks would just stand there and watch. Now they whipped out their phones and started recording. Smartphones were SPI's bane. In the old days, when someone said they saw a werewhatever, it was their word against a world that wondered where they'd stashed their tinfoil hat. Now, it was merely a matter of being in the right place at the right time. Contrary to what you might believe, there were very few supernaturals who couldn't be photographed. That made our job infinitely more difficult. That didn't even take into account what would happen if the supernatural who was being photographed or filmed was the human-eating variety. The result was usually the meal-to-be documenting their own deaths. SPI's cleanup team scooped up a lot of phones in addition to hosing down sidewalks—all under a sight-obscuring cloaking spell, of course.

Ian leaned in close. "Was this a portal?"

I continued to stare and shook my head. "Not by any definition I've ever heard of."

I'd recently added portal detection to my skill set. Though a "set" indicated you had more than one to begin with. I didn't. A portal was like a door you could walk through. In theory, distance didn't matter. The house had come from another world, so unless houses on Rake's world had legs, it hadn't stepped through anything. I had no clue what had happened here.

An officer approached us. "The fire may spread. You'll need to move back."

He was an elf. His ears were glamoured, but I could see the pointed tips.

"Elf," I told Rake quietly without moving my lips. There were non-SPI humans now sharing the sidewalk with us.

The elven officer's eyes widened when he spotted Rake. He recognized him even with the glamour that hid his goblin features. Probably every supernatural in the tristate area knew what Rake's human guise looked like. Most of all, they knew who and what he was, and respected (and sometimes feared) both.

Rake stepped forward and began speaking quickly to the elf, but careful to keep his voice down. Ian was right behind him. I stayed put. They were doing their thing; I was going to do mine. As a former NYPD homicide detective, Ian was still well known to those in the ranks. I couldn't hear what they were saying to the elf cop, but I didn't need to.

Moments later, Rake quickly crossed to where Kylie and I were. "We're going to speak with the fire chief. Ian knows him."

I nodded. "Good. I'll have a look around from here."

I knew what Rake meant, and he knew what I was talking about.

SPI had people in all levels of the NYPD, NYFD, and throughout the local government and beyond. They ran interference when supernatural events leaked out into the mortal world. Unfortunately, that happened more often than we would've liked. This wasn't a little leak; it was a conflagration probably visible from the International Space Station. Getting a publicly acceptable story in place now would save SPI a lot of trouble later.

I'd stayed put because I could do the most good scanning the crowd for what no one else would be able to see.

Our arsonist.

I tried to look around without being obvious about it, which was easier said than done.

In my opinion, someone wouldn't pull a building in from another world, then torch it, without staying around to watch. Even if they didn't need to be physically present to do whatever it was they'd done, they wouldn't be able to resist being here to see their work properly appreciated.

This was Rake's house on Rake's lot, within throwing distance of SPI HQ and our favorite watering hole. The house and location choice weren't an accident or coincidence. It was personal, a smack in our collective face.

Whoever was responsible for this was here. Watching the fire.

And probably watching us.

I briefly closed my eyes to try to block out the ordered chaos of the scene from the police, firefighters, and onlookers, and focus on what was intended to be less obvious. Onlookers or even a firefighter or police officer who was watching us.

When I slowly opened my eyes again, I saw I wasn't the only one.

I spotted several police officers scanning the crowd for anyone who was enjoying the blaze more than they should. Two of the officers were humans and the third a supernatural, another elf to be exact.

Rake was speaking with a man who I assumed was the fire chief. Ian was with him, but seemed to be doing the same thing as me—scanning the crowd for suspicious-looking characters.

My eyes were drawn up toward the night sky. Earlier, it had been cloudy with a funky kind of flashy lightning, almost like strobe lights. No rain had come of it. Now it was clear— at least of clouds.

Light the color of flame still flowed in waves in the sky above the burning building. The closest comparison I could draw was northern lights, except these were gold rather than the usual green. Northern lights didn't appear this far south; and if they did, they sure as heck wouldn't be doing their thing in the small patch of sky directly above a burning building.

I went back to scanning the crowd. Despite my seer skill, my actual eyes were only human. It was night, there was a building on fire, it was smoky, and there were enough flashing red and blue lights to induce the mother of all migraines, so it was next to impossible to see anyone acting suspiciously unless they were standing less than ten feet away.

Since I wasn't getting anywhere with my eyes, I opened my seer's senses. Over the years, I'd developed a knack for knowing when magic was in use or had recently been used. I started over, scanning the crowd beginning with those standing closest to our SPI group and working my way around.

Within seconds, I got my first clue that I was on to something: a rotten-egg stink. It was faint, but you couldn't miss it. The firemen battling the blaze might think it was something burning inside the building, but this went a couple steps beyond sulfur. This was brimstone. I'd had an unpleasant up-close experience getting a snoot full of the stuff. Up close as in a trip to an anteroom of Hell. That stench was imprinted in my nasal passages forever.

There had been a breeze when we'd walked from SPI to the Full Moon a couple of hours ago. Now there was wind. Yeah, a large fire made its own wind, but this was different.

When you weren't physically in Hell, a brimstone stink meant black magic had been recently worked. It didn't necessarily mean demonic work, but it was definitely the hallmark of black magic. The stink that clung to the practitioner who had worked it was more of a slimy sensation that imprinted on the emotions rather than any of the five senses. Otherwise normal people who were psychically sensitive would be able to detect a black magic practitioner and be repulsed by them on a subconscious level, instinctively wanting to put as much distance between themselves and that person as possible.

That precise sensation was coming from someone directly across from where we were standing, on the other side of the fire, and behind the barricades that mirrored our own. The source had positioned himself as close to the fire as he could get—and as far away as possible from me and my friends.

"Yeah, that's not a coincidence," I murmured.

"What?" Kenji asked.

"I may have just found our house-moving arsonist." I kept my voice soft and my body still. I also tried to keep my thoughts neutral and quiet. To do anything else would be like sending up a psychic flare telling this guy exactly where I was. And yes, I could tell this practitioner was male. I tentatively reached out just a little more. He was also a goblin.

A really angry goblin, as in a seething rage.

It didn't feel like a supernatural arsonist enjoying his work.

That wasn't a distinction I'd ever been able to make before. Male or female I could determine with about 90 percent accuracy. It was the goblin part that was new—and confusing. If I didn't know and could see that Rake was talking to the fire chief, I'd almost swear that he was...

I shook my head to clear it. The smoke must be getting to me.

I didn't want to risk alerting our mystery goblin, but I needed to get an actual look at this guy.

"I'll be right back," I murmured.

"Do you think that's a good..."

I didn't stick around to hear the rest. I knew what Kenji

was saying and thinking. No, it wasn't a good idea. It was a bad idea, not to mention risky, but my psychic hook was set, not in the practitioner himself, but in his aura. I had no intention of reeling him in. I was going to take up the line, so to speak, ever so gently, as I went to him. Or at least toward him. All I needed was to get a good look. We had psychic sketch artists at SPI who could take it from there. A quick mind link would be all it'd take for them to see what I'd seen, and voilà, instant mug shot.

I crossed the street and moved through the crowd toward Rake, maintaining the most tenuous of psychic contacts with the suspect as I went.

"Mac!"

I jumped, my concentration broken. It was only Ian, a shout to get my attention, but the spike of adrenaline had done its damage.

Psychically speaking, I was standing there as buck naked as the day I'd been born.

Oh crap.

The goblin's blow came like a punch to the side of my head, and the next thing I knew, I was falling in a sickening spin as the whole world went sideways, then dark.

I awoke to the acute realization that landing on concrete hurts. A lot.

Ian was picking me up off the sidewalk, so I must have only been out a few seconds.

Yay me.

In the sky, the golden northern lights continued to flow

and swirl, which did extremely unpleasant things to my head and stomach.

I knew what was coming up next, or at least what wanted to. I clenched my jaw, clutched my stomach, and firmly told the contents of my stomach to stay.

Ian had been around me long enough to know it, too. He held me up, but made sure my head was facing down and away from him. When nothing happened, I didn't know whether to be relieved or disappointed. Throwing up would have made me feel infinitely better, but I really didn't want to do it in public. I dimly wondered if I could make it to the Full Moon's ladies' room in time. At least I thought that was what I was thinking. Everything was still kinda whirly.

Then I saw something that instantly cleared my head.

Across the street, four firemen in those silver fire suits with respirators and air tanks were about to go into the building.

I squirmed out of Ian's arms to get a clearer view. "What the—" I froze. "Ian, Rake said there's no one in there. They're risking their lives for nothing. We have to stop them."

I glanced over to where Rake had been standing with the fire chief.

Rake's eyes had gone wide with disbelief, his face pale. Not because of seeing the firemen preparing to go in, but because of what he was now sensing.

Oh no. There *was* someone alive in there.

Rake's expression hardened, his lips narrowed with grim determination. He didn't need to say "I'm going in." His expression and stance said it loud and clear.

Yelling for Rake to stop wouldn't work, and it'd only draw attention to what he was about to do.

Rake moved quickly, darting behind a firetruck.

When he came out, I was the only one who could see him. Rake had cloaked and shielded himself—from view and from the fire—and had run right into that burning building.

I grabbed Ian's arm. "Rake ran in!"

Ian spat his go-to word for when an already bad situation just went completely and hopelessly sideways.

Normally, seeing your boyfriend run into a burning building would be cause for concern, if not panic.

My boyfriend wasn't normal.

He'd once jumped into a swirling pit of molten brimstone to save me, swimming in it as if it was a heated swimming pool, albeit one with a vortex at the center draining straight into Hell itself.

The barricades and the police standing in front of them kept me from getting any closer.

Ian and I just stood there. It wasn't like either one of us could run in there after him. Mortals melted, or were at least highly flammable.

Rake would come out when he'd done what he'd gone in to do.

3

Minutes that felt like an eternity later, Rake came out with a body over his shoulder. The firefighters were right behind him.

Everyone could see him now.

Rake had dropped his cloaking spell, but he was still glamoured as a human—as was the man over his shoulder.

I could tell he was a goblin.

The firefighters had gone in with respirators. Rake had gone in with naked lungs protected by magic, so he had to make a show of being at least mildly affected. Rule number one of being a supernatural trying to blend in with humans— don't be impervious to things that would kill a mortal.

Rake stumbled, going down on one knee, his face twisted in pain.

He wasn't acting.

I pushed past the police at the barricade and ran toward him. I dimly heard Ian shouting as he ran interference behind me.

Two of the firemen had taken the goblin from Rake and hustled them both over to the EMTs. When I got to him, Rake had an oxygen mask over his mouth and nose and was coughing. One look in his eyes confirmed he wasn't faking.

He was hurt—and he was afraid, not of anything he'd seen, but of what had happened.

Or rather, had not happened.

I'd only seen that type of fear from Rake once before. He couldn't talk and tell me, but I knew.

His magic had failed. Something or someone had interfered with his magic.

I had questions, but I couldn't ask any of them until we weren't surrounded by firefighters and the EMTs who didn't work for SPI, and while Rake was wheezing and hacking his lungs up.

He'd had enough magic to glamour himself and the man he'd carried out of the burning building. Glamours were small magic. Keeping the flames from a fully engulfed building from burning both of them to death had taken every last bit of strength Rake had.

The goblin was older than Rake, how much older I didn't know. It was difficult to tell with goblins. He was unconscious, but breathing.

Rake lifted the oxygen mask. "Keep us...together," he rasped, indicating the goblin.

"I'll take care of it." I pushed the mask back over his face. "Now shut up and *breathe*."

I knew what he meant. Rake wanted the first face the man

saw to be his, preferably his true goblin face, not the human glamour. If I'd been taken from a Renaissance-level world and plopped down in the middle of Manhattan with flashing emergency lights and skyscrapers soaring overhead, the shock would probably kill me. This poor guy needed to at least see a friendly face when he woke up. Fortunately, his clothing was dark and nondescript, so he didn't look like he'd just come from a Renfaire or costume party.

As a seer, I could detect auras. The goblin was a mage of a respectable level. He would have needed that much power to have avoided being burned to a crisp before Rake had gotten him out.

An ambulance pulled onto the sidewalk, followed by another less than a minute later. The logos on the sides indicated city ambulances, but I recognized the paramedics.

They were from SPI. That meant the ambulances were ours, too.

Minutes before, one of the paramedics had been at my party. Calvin had been an army medic in Iraq. He'd added a navy windbreaker to the clothes he'd worn to the party and blended right in. He was helping load the unconscious mage into the ambulance. Since joining SPI, Cal had learned the physiologies of our world's more common supernatural species. The mage was in good hands.

"Go tell Cal his patient's a goblin," I told Ian.

Ian reluctantly went to deliver the message. I knew he didn't want to leave me after what'd happened.

Rake grabbed my hand and pushed something into it. I only had a moment to glance down at it before Rake folded my fingers closed into a fist.

A broken chain attached to a pulsing red stone.

"Gethen...quick," he rasped, right before he passed out.

I got into the first ambulance with Rake for the short trip to SPI headquarters, where we had a trauma unit that rivaled any New York hospital. When your employees fought monsters and powerful mages and supernatural criminals, their injuries would do more than raise eyebrows at the neighborhood ER. Ms. Sagadraco made sure we had only the best medical care available to us.

Before we were even a block away from the fire, my phone came back to life.

I did what Rake had asked and called Gethen Nazar.

It was a predictably short conversation.

Gethen was Rake's chief of security. Normally, he'd be called a bodyguard, but Rake's "normal" had jumped out the nearest window when he'd reluctantly accepted the goblin governorship. Besides, bodyguard was singular. Chief of security meant Gethen was in charge of the other unfortunates who had the unenviable job of keeping Rake among the living. But since Rake had been spending the evening at my birthday party within throwing distance of SPI HQ, and had been surrounded by SPI's best and baddest agents and commandos, Gethen had reluctantly taken the night off at Rake's insistence.

In Gethen's mind, that had made us responsible for Rake's safety.

In Gethen's opinion, we had failed in our duty.

He hadn't said that on the phone or even alluded to it, but I got the vibe loud and clear.

It was well after midnight, and after talking to Gethen, my birthday fun was over in more ways than one.

Rake stirred and opened his eyes. He looked around in a panic and started coughing again.

"Your mage is in the ambulance right behind us," I told him, gripping one of his hands in both of mine. "Ian's with him. He's going to be okay." I softened my voice and squeezed his hand. "We've got this, hon. Just breathe and try to relax."

Rake's body was wracked with a violent fit of coughing that arched his back off the stretcher. With a gasp, his eyes rolled up in his head, as he went limp and still.

"Rake?" I tightened my grip on his hand in panic. "Cal!"

"He's fine," Cal hurried to assure me. The beeping of Rake's heart monitor confirmed it, but my own heart pounding against my ribs wasn't buying it. "He's breathing on his own." Cal repositioned Rake's oxygen mask. "The coughing makes it sound worse than it is. He just passed out."

I squeezed my eyes shut against the sting of tears and nodded.

Take your own advice, Mac. Relax and breathe.

When I opened them, it was to a concerned Cal. "Ian told me you took a spill and wants me to check you over. He's right. You don't look so good."

"Gee, thanks. Just what every girl wants to hear on her birthday."

"I'm serious. What happened?"

I gave him the short version. It was all my throbbing head had left me capable of doing.

"I need to check for a concussion," he said when I'd finished. "Hold still."

I heard the click and I groaned. "Not the pen light."

"It'll only take a second." Cal flicked the light from one eye to the other.

Thankfully, the driver chose that moment to flip off the lights and siren. Then he pushed a button on the console to activate what I called the "these are not the droids you're looking for" signal. The mages in our Research and Development department had installed them in all our agency vehicles. One of our ambulances could go screaming down a street, and people would actually ignore it—even more than New Yorkers normally ignored such things.

The R&D mages had also done some nifty work disguising the five vehicle-accessible entrances into SPI's underground headquarters. Three looked like the entrances to private parking garages, and the other two were what appeared to be loading docks.

Less than half a block later, the gates opened into one of SPI's fake garages.

Dr. Barbara Carey and a trauma team met us at SPI's subterranean loading dock doors. She was the lady in charge of our medical center. Her word was law.

Only when Rake and the mage were in their care did I let go of Rake's hand. After telling Dr. Carey that Rake needed to be near the mage, I headed toward the waiting room, but Ian and Cal appeared on either side of me, each taking an elbow, and steered me to a treatment bay where one of SPI's doctors waited by a gurney that right about now looked like the most comfortable thing ever.

I relented. A nap sounded really good.

Alas, sleep was not to be.

Dr. Stephens had deemed me to be concussion free, though he strongly suggested that I get some rest.

That was not to be, either.

Gethen Nazar had arrived upstairs and was being escorted down to the medical center. Rake was still unconscious, and I carried a shiny, red rock in my pocket that might shed some light on what had happened to him inside that burning house. Rake had asked me to give it to Gethen. The sooner I did that, the quicker we could start getting some answers.

After leaving me in Dr. Stephens's capable care, Ian went upstairs to the agent bullpen to fight some fires of his own. The recordings from SPI's neighborhood surveillance cameras needed to be examined for the hours prior to the event and the electricity going out. I'd be going over the same tapes later for any sign of my goblin attacker. Also, our own investigation would need to be coordinated with that of the city police and fire departments. Our allies inside the various city departments would be alerted to ensure the incident appeared to be nothing more than a typical building fire. I had no clue what they were doing about the fact that said building had burned on a lot that'd been vacant for months. The solution to that dilemma was way above my ability and pay grade.

I was sitting in the waiting area when Gethen came through the medical center doors and began walking down the hall toward me, I didn't say a word. I just looked at him and threw my hands up in what had become our sign for "Yeah, Rake went off the rails again. I did what I could."

Gethen replied with his usual eye roll, directed at his wayward boss, not me.

We'd done this dance entirely too many times recently.

Rake was gonna do what Rake was gonna do, and he wasn't about to let anyone stop him.

"How is he?" Gethen asked when he got close enough.

"They're working on him now. Calvin said smoke inhalation."

Gethen frowned. "That shouldn't be possible."

I ran a hand over my face. "I know. He was cloaked and shielded when he went in. He was in there less than two minutes. When he came out, his glamour was up, but his shields were down. Something happened to his magic, and I don't think he knew what it was. He told me to call you"—I started digging into my jeans pocket—"and give you this."

Gethen looked before he took, and that look told me I probably shouldn't have let that stone stay in my pocket for a minute, let alone an hour. But I hadn't had anywhere else to put it, and my thigh didn't feel like it'd been absorbing evil, so I chalked it up to yet another unavoidable hazard of working for SPI.

Like Rake, Gethen was a dark mage. Also like Rake, he hadn't survived the dangers that went with his chosen career path without developing a finely tuned sense of caution.

"So, what is it?" I asked, wiping my hand on my jeans and wondering if there was such a thing as psychic Purell.

Gethen's lips had gone from his usual narrowed in annoyance to vanished without a trace. He quickly hissed a few words in Goblin of what I recognized as a high-powered containment spell, and the red stone stopped pulsing.

Yeah, I definitely shouldn't have shoved that necklace in my pocket. I blamed my poor decision-making on a psychic fist to the head.

"You don't want to know what it is," Gethen told me.

"*Want* doesn't have anything to do with it. If I didn't *need* to know, I wouldn't have asked."

We'd done this dance before, too. Though sparring would be a better description.

Gethen was a goblin. While I knew he was simply doing what goblins did, it didn't make it any less annoying. If you wanted information out of one, you needed to go find yourself a crowbar.

I blew out my breath. "You're doing your job; I'm trying to do mine." I didn't say "but you're not making it easy." Gethen knew what he was doing and how little I liked it. What I needed to know was why he was doing it.

"The pendant is Khrynsani," he said.

"And . . ?"

"I take it Rake hasn't told you about them."

"Not much, other than they're basically the goblin version of Nazis. It seems I need to know more now. Rake's unconscious." I gave him a tight smile. "You're not." I left the "yet" unspoken. We both knew that as an itty-bitty thing, physically as well as psychically, I couldn't put a dent in any piece or part of him, but I was tired of getting the runaround, and was just tired, period.

"Very well. This"—he dangled the stone by its chain—"is what in your military would be used as a dog tag. With it we can identify the Khrynsani it belongs to."

"You're losing me. The mage was the only one in the house."

"The only one alive. I suspect this particular Khrynsani's body will be found in the rubble once it cools enough for anyone to get in. Judging from the glow before I applied a stasis spell, this contains said Khrynsani's soul." Gethen regarded the slowly spinning stone with a wicked little smile.

I *really* should not have put that thing in my pocket. "What?" I managed.

"Either Lord Danescu or the mage he brought out killed the Khrynsani and imprisoned his soul inside. The Khrynsani call these lifestones. They all wear one. They were created for such a purpose, but the dying Khrynsani's soul would have fled into it only if he knew that this receptacle would remain safe until his comrades could collect it. He had to know, or at least suspect, that it would fall into our hands, so I don't believe he went willingly."

"He was shoved in there?"

"That would be an apt description."

I'd been walking around with a Nazi goblin's soul in my pocket.

It was a good thing I was in the medical center, because I was feeling a wee bit woozy again.

Then I remembered that Rake had made me take it, and woozy turned to angry. "Rake gave me a dead goblin's soul?"

"The soul should be securely locked inside," Gethen assured me.

"Should?"

"Lord Danescu could not risk losing consciousness while the lifestone was on him, in case the soul still had the strength to escape. He would have been possessed."

"And it'd be no biggie if *I* was possessed."

"You are human and a female. The Khrynsani would not have possessed you. Lord Danescu would have known this."

"So I'm not good enough to be possessed?"

"In the Khrynsani's opinion it would be like possessing…"

I narrowed my eyes. "A what?"

"A sub-creature. That is a Khrynsani opinion," he assured me. "It not an opinion held by either Lord Danescu, myself, or any civilized goblin."

I was placated. For now. Maybe.

"Rather than possess another," Gethen continued, "this Khrynsani will attempt to escape when we extract him for interrogation."

"You said normally his buddies would collect his…soul jewelry. For what?"

"The Khrynsani consider physical bodies to be both disposable and interchangeable. His temple brothers would locate a suitable donor body, extract the soul inside, and imprison it in a receptacle for future use as fuel for powering large spells. Once the donor body was vacant, they would release their brother's soul into it."

I was officially beyond words.

Zombie Nazi goblins.

My skin crawled from my scalp clean down to my toes.

Gethen had said I didn't want to know. Did I believe him? Nooo.

"May I see the man he saved from the fire?" I dimly heard Gethen ask.

"Yeah, yeah," I said in a daze. "Sure. Dr. Carey won't let anyone in with him, but there's a glass wall into a monitoring room next door. I can see about getting us in there."

"Good enough."

The room looked like one in a hospital's intensive care unit. There were two beds. Rake was in one, with the goblin mage in the other.

I was pretty sure the room was soundproof, but I kept my voice down anyway. "Rake's weak from the smoke inhalation and whatever happened to him in the fire. Dr. Carey wants to keep him sedated and intubated for a few hours so he can rest and regain his strength. The mage's injuries are similar to Rake's, but more severe since he was in the building longer." I paused. "That was another thing Rake asked me to do—make sure they were kept together. I don't think Rake wanted him waking up in a completely unfamiliar place. Ideally, Rake will be up and able to be at the mage's bedside when he regains consciousness."

"His name is Tulis Minic."

Now we were getting somewhere, though not very quickly if I had to keep pulling information out of Gethen piece by piece.

"Who is he?"

"The Danescu family security mage. My counterpart in the goblin capital."

"Has he ever been here before?" I asked.

"He has not."

"Poor guy," I whispered.

"And he only speaks Goblin, which is no doubt why Lord Danescu insisted that they remain together."

"Does he know you?"

"He does."

I let out a breath I wasn't aware I'd been holding. Dr. Carey had assured us that Rake would be awake long before

Tulis, but I felt better knowing Gethen would be there to keep him from freaking out just in case. SPI's trauma center was set up to handle almost anything, but that didn't include an injured and panicked goblin dark mage of Gethen's level. Predators were most dangerous when they were wounded and felt trapped.

"I take it you're staying here until Rake—"

"I will not be moved from this spot."

"Well, we can get you a chair. Unlike the ones in human hospitals, our chairs are comfy and even fold out into beds."

Gethen's eyes remained on Rake's still form. "That will not be necessary."

His expression clearly said he'd made a mistake leaving Rake alone tonight, and that mistake would not be repeated. Ever.

Gethen Nazar had officially gone from being Rake's bodyguard to Rake's shadow.

Oh joy.

4

Dr. Carey removed Rake's breathing tube two hours later, deeming him able to breathe on his own well enough to let him wake up. The IV was disconnected, and before long, Rake began to stir. Yes, he'd known where he was being taken before he'd passed out, but logic, either of thought or action, wasn't the first thing to come back online when you'd been out for a while. And when you were a dark mage… Well, Dr. Carey had a nice medical center, and she wanted to keep it and her staff more or less intact.

Hence, I was sitting by Rake's bed again holding his hand when he opened his eyes.

Rake gave me a groggy smile. It was a beautiful thing to see—at least as much as I could see through eyes that'd suddenly gone all misty on me. Then he saw a grim Gethen

Nazar standing over my shoulder. I didn't need to look for myself to know Gethen was grim. It was his perpetual state of being.

"I'm in trouble," Rake rasped.

"You are not in trouble, sir," Gethen assured him. "You are, however, under guard every hour of every day in perpetuity."

"Like I said, trouble."

I cleared my throat. "Speaking of trouble, I gave Gethen that red rock with the dead Khrynsani's soul inside."

Rake gave a little wince. "Sorry about that. I didn't have a choice."

I gave him a little dose of guilt. "Um-hmm. So Gethen said."

Gethen pulled up a chair beside me and sat. It was about time. He'd been literally standing guard for the past four hours. While I was sure he could've stood there for as long as it took, like a good soldier, he was now sitting and resting while he could. I had a sinking feeling he knew something we didn't, and it had everything to do with that Khrynsani lifestone that was now in his pocket.

Rake's eyes widened as another layer of sedation lifted. "Tulis?"

"He took in a little more smoke than you did, plus a knife in the ribs." I nodded to the far side of the room. "He's right over there. Dr. Carey said the blade missed anything vital, and that he's gonna be fine. He just needs rest."

Rake turned his head to look. "I need to talk to him."

"We'd all like some answers, but for now, Dr. Carey's calling the shots. That includes you. We need to know what happened, but Tulis isn't the only one who needs rest." I glanced over to where Dr. Carey stood in the hall watching us like an overprotective hawk. "She's only gonna let us talk to you for so long."

Rake's expression hardened.

Oh boy, here we go again.

When he spoke, his voice was strong and sure—and stubborn—with no trace of damage. "That will have to change."

Within half an hour, we were all ensconced in the monitoring room next door, which had been hastily converted into a conference room by pulling in more chairs. Rake had insisted on being able to watch Tulis, and Dr. Carey had insisted on being able to watch Rake. His only concession to medical care was the wheelchair he was presently sitting in, and the monitoring equipment on a little rolling cart next to him.

The three of us had been joined by SPI founder Vivienne Sagadraco and her second-in-command, Alain Moreau. Mr. Moreau was also my manager.

And a vampire.

But when the founder of the agency was a multi-millennia-old, fire-breathing dragon, having a centuries-old French vampire manager was downright normal. Ms. Sagadraco's human form looked like a petite and elegant socialite in her late sixties, and Mr. Moreau could've passed for Anderson Cooper's even paler twin brother.

Right now, Rake was beating himself up for not sensing Tulis sooner.

"If it had been a normal situation, you would have," I

told him. "Rake, someone picked up your house from *another planet* and dropped it into the middle of Manhattan. Have you ever seen anything like that in your life?"

"No."

"Gethen?"

The goblin mage shook his head.

"Exactly," I said. "It was magic, and it was *huge*. I'd think the distortion from that magic would be equally huge. Tulis is alive—thanks to you—and he's going to stay that way. You did everything you could. Is it possible the distortion was what sapped your magic?"

"I don't think so. As soon as I stepped across the threshold, I felt my power being pulled away, toward the middle of the house—where Tulis and the Khrynsani agent were."

"And when it was 'pulled away,' your shields started failing, leaving you in a burning house with nothing but your bare naked lungs."

"Yes."

"And you didn't consider letting four fully equipped and highly trained firemen do their jobs?"

Rake just looked at me like he didn't understand the question.

I sighed. "Of course, you didn't." That was my Rake, brave to the point of suicide. I couldn't decide which urge was stronger: kiss him or smack him upside the head.

Though after I told them about getting attacked, Rake might have similar impulses about me.

Time to fess up. "Before we go any further, Ms. Sagadraco, I should probably report on what happened to me."

Rake went very still.

"Hey, you were unconscious," I told him, in what I thought was a fine excuse. "And when you weren't unconscious, you were groggy. I just didn't want to have to repeat myself."

"Right."

Ms. Sagadraco sat a little straighter. "What happened, Agent Fraser?"

I told her. However, I neglected to put the blame on Ian for breaking my concentration. Any goblin who was powerful enough to potentially be involved in bringing a house here from another world certainly had enough mojo under the hood to magically knock out my lights any time he danged well pleased. He'd probably been waiting for me to get closer before he did anything. The more I thought about it, the more likely it was that I wasn't the only one who'd wanted to get a good look at their opponent. When Ian had called out to me, the goblin probably figured he wasn't going to get an up-close-and-personal shot, so he'd best take what he could get. Looking at it that way, my partner had probably saved my life. And even if he hadn't, he had no way of knowing that I was hot on a trail. I really needed to come up with a way to signal that kind of thing.

Rake was giving me a level look throughout my entire report. Goblins had raised white lies—and every other color—to a fine art. He knew I wasn't telling them everything. And it didn't help matters that I was a bad liar.

"If you encountered him again, would you be able to recognize him with your seer senses?" Rake asked.

I resisted the urge to rub my jaw, which had been the first of my pieces and parts to slam into the concrete sidewalk. "Oh, I can guarantee it."

"Good." With that, Rake let it drop. I knew it wouldn't stay dropped.

Gethen leaned forward. "The Khrynsani, sir. What happened?"

"He was dead at Tulis's feet in the hall outside my study," Rake said. "I had to reach Tulis before the firemen. They would have seen that he wasn't human, and he wouldn't have known the silver-clad beings walking through fire didn't mean him harm. They wouldn't have made it out alive."

Rake paused and tried to swallow. I had water ready for him.

"How about just give us the *Reader's Digest* version for now," I told him.

"The what?" he rasped.

"Short version now. Details later."

Rake nodded. "By the time I got to Tulis, he was unconscious beside the Khrynsani agent. I took the lifestone off the body. My magic was nearly gone, so I dropped the cloak so I could disguise Tulis as human." He paused and drew a few ragged breaths. "I didn't run into the firemen until I'd reached the front door. They didn't see anything they shouldn't."

"The body should still be in the rubble," Moreau noted. "Lord Danescu, you said you found Tulis and the body near the center of the house?"

"Yes."

Moreau stood and took out his phone. "I'll have the remains found and brought here," he told Ms. Sagadraco. He turned to leave.

Gethen spoke. "Mr. Moreau, I need to go with whoever

retrieves that body. Whatever affected Lord Danescu's magic was nearby. I need to find it before anyone else does."

"With the intention of bringing it to our labs for study?"

"But of course."

Alain Moreau hadn't lived as many centuries as he had by making assumptions. Gethen Nazar had loyalties, and they weren't to SPI. It might have been his boss's house, taken from his boss's world, and dropped on his boss's vacant lot, but this world and especially this city was SPI's responsibility.

This wasn't just Rake's problem, now it was ours.

5

We were confident that Rake wasn't going anywhere anytime soon, if only because Tulis was still unconscious, and Rake wasn't about to leave him alone until he was awake.

But when it came to Rake, you didn't take chances. Gethen had called in two of his staff security mages to stand guard—one in Rake's room, the other guarding the only door in or out. Our agents had the exits to the medical center covered.

Rake got the message.

When we arrived at the scene, it was apparent that Vivienne Sagadraco had been pulling strings. My seer vision told me that half of the two dozen or so individuals inside the barricades were supernaturals. Most of those were on the team going through the embers. Five of them were from SPI's lab. Kenji Hayashi was slowly walking through the rubble, intent on the small screen of a handheld device. All were focused on their tasks.

We had one thing in our favor as far as keeping the situation from going up in flames like Rake's house had—the mortal authorities' refusal to believe anything that smacked of the supernatural, and the reluctance on the part of their investigators to include any such explanation in their reports. No one wanted to be the wack-job who believed in woo-woo. And certainly no one wanted their superiors to order a psych evaluation for anyone who did.

SPI had raised low-key to a high art. Ian, Gethen, and I were posing as insurance adjusters, and were dressed much like the NYPD folks on the scene in jeans and dark windbreakers. We wore ID on lanyards around our necks with photos that matched our glamours.

The NYPD arson investigator in charge of the site would be expecting us—the glamoured versions. Gethen appeared to be shorter than his actual height, with dark blond hair and blue eyes. Being a mage, he'd taken care of doing his own glamour. The mages in our R&D department had developed amulets that they could pre-charge with a time-released disguise that was undetectable by anyone except seers. Ian and I were wearing their work underneath our shirts.

Criminals aren't the only ones who need glamours. To keep from freaking out their human neighbors, supernaturals need to wear a glamour or some other magical disguise to hide what they are. Elves have it easy; they just have their ears to contend with. The rest of their bodies look pretty much human, albeit an inhumanly perfect human. But with all the kinds of plastic surgery available now, even humans can look as good as elves. When they came here, elves spread out and settled all over the place. However, a lot of them gravitated toward places like Los Angeles and New York to become actors, singers, models, and dancers. If your favorite celeb looks or sounds too good to be human, chances are they're not.

Criminals have always had a thing for disguises. While humans are stuck with things like hats, wigs, glasses, and fake noses to keep from being picked out of a lineup later, supernaturals have a nearly limitless selection to choose from, that limit being their ability to produce a glamour themselves or pay a mage to create one and place it in an accessory that the supernatural wears all the time, such as a watch or ring. The spell needs to be recharged every so often, and the mage gets paid again. Glamour mages can make some serious money. If you're rich enough, you can basically design your own face and body. The look you've always dreamed of can be yours. Glamour mages are a lot like plastic surgeons, though. Some do beautiful work, others utterly suck. It's buyer beware, and always ask for references.

An NYPD officer was standing guard at the police barriers. He checked our IDs and let us through. He was an elf, not human. Like ourselves, he was glamoured to pass as what he wanted mortal New Yorkers to see, an average-looking human man. To fit in with mortals, you had to blend in and be someone that no one gave a second glance, and barely a first.

We were inside the crime scene perimeter, but others weren't going to be allowed anywhere near it. Once investigators were finished with their work, the lot would be cleared, the debris hauled away by SPI contractors and destroyed.

The press was behind the barricades across the street recording everything with cameras that could zoom in close enough to count the pores on your nose. Hence our glamours. Gethen was well known as Rake Danescu's bodyguard among the press that covered the lives of New York's hoity-toity set. I was even more well known to the paparazzi as Rake's serious girlfriend. Ian was just trying to go through life being as unnoticed as possible.

Thanks to the electrical outage caused by the event, there was no video of Rake Danescu, billionaire and ex-playboy, coming out of a burning building with a man over his shoulder.

But there had been hundreds of eager eyewitnesses.

Rake was being hailed as a hero in the press and public.

It was driving everyone in both groups nuts that Rake and the mystery man he had saved were nowhere to be found. They hadn't been admitted to any of the local hospitals. Witnesses had seen them loaded into ambulances and watched those ambulances drive away, but oddly enough, no one remembered the company or hospital name on the side.

Score another point for SPI's R&D mage geeks.

But the thing that had set the press to salivating was that until the fire, this had been a vacant lot. Rake Danescu's vacant lot. And no one was drooling more than Baxter Clayton.

An investigative reporter for one of the local network affiliates, Baxter had been trying to get dirt on Rake for years. When you'd once owned a high-class sex club, people didn't have to dig far to hit pay dirt. Baxter had no clue that Rake wasn't human—and we were here to make sure he didn't find anything to tell him otherwise.

Ian made a beeline for a man of average height and unusual aura. Gethen and I followed. The arson investigator was a firemage. This guy's aura was the color of flames. SPI had several firemages on staff, and one of them was among those presently going through the blackened rubble of what used to be Rake's house. There were actually a few walls left standing, but most of the rubble was just that, piles of blackened wood and stone.

The fire had been extinguished, but there were still hot spots. A couple of firemen were working on those to keep any embers from flaring back up. The brimstone stink from last night was still hanging in the air, but now my olfactory experience was being raised to whole new levels of nasty. The only thing worse than brimstone stink was wet brimstone stink.

We began picking our way through the rubble. We wore boots developed by SPI's R&D folks that looked like what arson investigators wore to a crime scene, but were infinitely more fireproof. Our director of demonology, Martin DiMatteo, routinely made field trips to Hell, and as a mere human, needed the extra protection. My tootsies appreciated their temporary safehouses. Since there were still a few walls remaining upright, we were also wearing hard hats.

"Thankfully, our building materials are primitive by Earth standards," Gethen said quietly from beside me. "Wood, brick, and stone."

I also kept my voice down. "Rake calls home 'the Seven Kingdoms.' Doesn't your world have a name?"

"While we have abundant magic, our technology—if you can call it that—is such that we have never seen our world or any other from space, so no one has ever seen a need to name it. The elves and goblins of our world have spent millennia trying to annihilate each other. For either to admit that they share anything such as a world that they cannot forcefully take from the other... Well, it simply doesn't bear thinking about."

I nodded slowly. In a strange and twisted way, that made sense.

"If someone went to all the trouble to bring a building from...your home, why would they torch it once they got it here? A Renaissance-style house popping up on a vacant New York lot makes one heck of a statement, but not if you immediately burn it down."

"I believe we will discover that the fire was an accident," Gethen said. "Or an unforeseen result of whatever magic was used to bring it here."

Before we'd left, I'd asked Rake what exactly we were looking for. He'd given me a typically cryptic goblin answer: He didn't know, but chances were good that Gethen or I would know it when we saw it.

Suddenly there was a flurry of activity near the center of the ruins.

Ian started toward them. "They've found a body."

Oh boy, had they ever.

I'd only seen a burnt-to-a-crisp corpse once before—a goblin lawyer who had been baked inside a cookie oven by a disgruntled client.

This body was also a goblin. But this time, it was worse.

I stood close enough to see, but far enough away to be

downwind from most of the stench that'd filled the air once the searchers had uncovered him.

The body was blackened and burned—with the vivid exception of an area over the goblin's heart that had been tattooed with two bright red serpents twining around each other.

"Khrynsani," Gethen hissed from over my shoulder.

"Is that normal, for some tattoos not to burn?" I asked the medical examiner who had made the discovery.

"No," she said, snapping on a pair of blue latex gloves. "It is not."

Dr. Anika Van Daal ought to know. She had more experience than every doctor in New York combined.

Dr. Van Daal was a vampire and mage, and a true New Yorker. She'd been here since 1625, when the city had been taken from the Dutch by the British and the name changed from New Amsterdam to New York.

She'd gone from midwife to the city's first licensed female doctor. Every few decades, she "retired" from one position and took another. She'd been in her mid-twenties when she'd been turned, so she didn't stand out when she went back to school after one of her retirements to catch up on the latest medical advances. She'd learned to glamour and glamour well, aging her glamour along with what would be expected in a human. As a result, she'd never had problems blending in or with being found out.

As a mage, she could place a glamour on a dead supernatural that would remain until the body was turned over to the family, or if it was unclaimed, until it was cremated or buried by the city. Dr. Van Daal wouldn't need to do that here. She had a body bag ready to receive the dead goblin for transport back to SPI.

Rake and Gethen, along with SPI's resident necromancer Bert Ferguson, had a few questions for the departed. I was not looking forward to that.

"When a supplicant is accepted into the Khrynsani brotherhood, they are tattooed with the order's mark," Gethen was saying. "It cannot be removed by any means, including fire."

We had no problem leaving Dr. Van Daal to her work. The Khrynsani was only one of the things we'd come to find. The other was still buried somewhere in the blackened rubble around us.

Even if we'd known what we were looking for, I didn't think it would've been much help.

I was standing roughly in the center of the structure. I turned in a slow circle. My human senses were uncomfortable here to say the least. The smoke stung my eyes, and it'd be a long time before I got the brimstone stink and oily taste of smoke out of my nose and mouth. Then there was the noise. This was an active crime scene. Phones and cameras worked now. The danger and the excitement were over for the gathered crowd, but not the insatiable curiosity. Large groups of people plus curiosity equaled noise. Yes, it was in the background, but it was still distracting, especially the press's shouted questions to anyone working the site who might be willing to stroll over to the barricades and answer them.

Last, but certainly not least, it was hot. Last night's fire hadn't been normal. It'd burned hotter then, so it was hot now.

I wiped the sweat off my forehead with the back of my

hand, turned away from the street and its crowds, and stepped behind one of the remaining walls for enough peace and quiet so I could work. I squeezed my eyes shut against the drying heat and did my best to block out the other distractions as I opened my seer senses.

I didn't send out any psychic feelers; I was merely still, leaving my senses open to whatever lay in the rubble beneath my boots.

Gradually, I became aware of a low, pulsing hum.

I opened my eyes, my attention drawn to the outskirts of the search area. Only one investigator was searching there.

He was glamoured like the other supernatural NYPD investigators, but I couldn't see through his disguise, as I could theirs. It shifted and flowed, and as I stood still, watching and listening, the briefest of openings gave me enough of a read to know that he was not merely a goblin, he was *the* goblin.

Last night, he'd been angry. Now he had anxiety and desperation piled on top of that.

And the vague impression of Rake was still there, though this guy was obviously not Rake, since Rake was in bed at SPI HQ.

I froze. "Gethen," I whispered. He wasn't far away, but he wasn't close, either. I was counting on his goblin hearing right now.

Gethen's head was down as he searched and moved carefully through the rubble. At my whispered call, he stopped, but he didn't lift his head, instead cutting only his eyes toward me.

Good. He knew something was wrong.

I flicked my eyes toward the glamoured goblin.

Who was now standing straight and tall and staring at both of us.

Crap.

Things went entirely too fast after that—those things being Gethen and the goblin. It was all over before I could even get my clunky boots to move.

The goblin hadn't been able to see through my glamour, but when I'd opened my seer senses, it'd must have been like waving a red flag at a bull. The two of us were behind a wall, visible to no one except Gethen. The goblin gathered his power in an instant, and everything went into that slow motion that gives you a sneak peek into what it was going to feel like to be reduced to a damp spot on burnt ground.

An acid-green fireball raced toward me. I knew I couldn't dodge in time, and if I tried, it would merely dodge with me like a heat-seeking missile. Just before impact, Gethen dove in front of me, hands out like a soccer goalie. A red glow was radiating out from them like twin shields, not only blocking the fireball, but sending it back at its launcher. His shoulder clipped me, and we both went down in a tumble of ash and soot.

Just before he would have been incinerated by his own fireball, the goblin touched a cuff on his wrist. There was a blinding flash of light, and when I could see again, the goblin was gone.

When he vanished, so did the fireball.

I lay sprawled in shock.

Gethen helped me to my feet. "Is that who you saw last night?"

I rubbed my upper arm, which had taken the brunt of my less than light landing. "Yeah. That was him. Thank you."

Ian and two of our agents ran around the wall to where we were. Ian didn't have his gun out, but there was a golden glow coming from beneath the collar of his windbreaker. Lugh's Spear had sensed the trouble and the goblin who had brought it, and it wanted a piece of the action. Maybe next time. I had a sinking feeling there was going to be one.

Gethen released his grip on my arm. "She had a visitor," he told Ian.

"The goblin mage from last night," I clarified. "Seems he's looking for the same thing we are. We need to find it. Now."

At first, it looked like just another hot spot with its orangey-gold glow.

Gethen crouched next to the light flickering from beneath a pile of blackened boards, his hands held out in front of him as if he were warming them against a fire. "It is magic most alien."

Ian and I joined him. Whatever was under those boards glowed like fire, but it didn't radiate any heat.

"Is it safe to uncover it?" Ian asked Gethen.

"I am not sensing any malice."

"You talk about it like it's alive," I noted.

"Life takes many forms, Lady Makenna."

The three of us put on gloves and carefully cleared the boards away to expose a crystal, its interior flickering with what looked like tongues of flame.

He softly hissed what I'd come to recognize as his go-to Goblin cuss word when a situation took an abrupt turn for the worse.

"You recognize it?" Ian asked him.

"Oh yes."

"Is it dangerous?" I whispered.

Gethen actually winced. "That depends."

6

When you worked for SPI's labs and were out in the field, you were always prepared to contain and carry. Whether it be organic, inorganic, or some funky thing that had been spawned somewhere in between, these folks had to bag it, tag it, and get it back to the lab without setting off a catastrophe of Biblical proportions.

Our lab techs' motto: We are professionals. Do *not* try this at home.

There wasn't much that fazed our lab field teams, and they were brave to a fault. Still, right now, since they were dealing with a crystal that might have been responsible for bringing a house here from another planet, there was a silent round robin going of: "You touch it."/"No, *you* touch it."

Our people would have picked it up eventually. To their credit, they even had the containment box open and ready. But before they could choose their sacrificial lamb, Gethen Nazar simply reached around them, picked up the rock, and shoved it in the box.

As per procedure, the lab techs thoroughly explored the immediate area surrounding any newfound strangeness. Very often the much-needed answers to some life or death questions weren't found in the object itself, but in what was around it. Since the entire site was going to be scrubbed clean, no one was going to risk leaving anything important behind.

They had taken photos, lots of photos, before they'd done their round-robin of passing the crystal buck. Those photos included the crystal and what surrounded it—a rectangle of what appeared to be metal that had been burnt down to slag.

"Size-wise, it looks like a piece of carry-on luggage that'd been laid on its side," I pointed out. "The little ridge of slag is even rounded where the corners would be, and it has the outline of what looks like a handle. Do your people have little suitcases on wheels?" I asked Gethen, only half kidding.

"No, we do not."

The crystal had been in the exact center, resting on top of what looked like a thin layer of the same slag. There had been nothing on the crystal itself. After we'd cleared away the debris, the crystal had been pristine, as if the flames inside the stone had burned away any ash that had attempted to sully its flickering perfection.

Gethen had hinted at it being some form of life.

I was starting to agree. If flickering could look smug, this thing was entirely too pleased with itself.

Getting the body and crystal back to SPI headquarters without the press tracking us like a pack of bloodhounds buzzed on Red Bull was quite the trick. Since the ambulance had gotten away with Rake and Tulis last night, one of the network affiliates had dispatched a helicopter and cameraman to track any vehicle their person on the ground told them to follow.

The SPI van, disguised as one from the city medical examiner's office, drove into one underground garage, activated its "cloaking device," popped invisible out the other side to quickly cross the street into one of the private parking garages that hid the entrance to headquarters, and the press was successfully foiled again.

We were on the receiving end of an even bigger surprise once we arrived on the third level of the headquarters complex where SPI's labs were located.

Rake was waiting for us, and at his side in a wheelchair was Tulis Minic, conscious and looking none the worse for wear. I knew mages could make short work of healing themselves, but dang. Then again, this was the guy who had killed a Khrynsani mage, then shoved his soul into a necklace while he'd been trapped inside a burning house that'd been brought here from another world.

Despite his mild-mannered appearance, if that didn't make him a badass, I didn't know what would.

Since Dr. Carey was hovering protectively nearby, I had a feeling the wheelchair was her doing. The mage looked like he could stand and walk just fine on his own. But then again, with goblins, looks were always deceiving, and they liked it that way.

Rake took care of the introductions—and translated for

Tulis from Goblin to English as the mage spoke in a voice still raspy from smoke.

"Pardon me for not rising or shaking hands," Rake translated.

Tulis cast a weak smile at Dr. Carey as he continued.

"My dear doctor won't allow it," Rake said for him. "I'm afraid I'm pushing the limits of her tolerance by even being out of bed." He glanced down the hall to where the gurney with the body bag was being wheeled into the lab for Bert's examination.

"I see you found him," Rake noted with satisfaction, speaking for himself now. "When Mr. Ferguson is ready, Gethen and I can secure the room and question our deceased guest."

Dr. Carey started to object, but Rake raised a hand. "Your concern is duly noted and appreciated, Dr. Carey. We don't have the luxury of time. We must question this Khrynsani. I assure you that I am well enough to do what must be done."

"We will not be taking any undue risks," Gethen assured her. "We have arranged with Director Sagadraco for two members of my staff to be present for additional security. Lord Danescu *will* be safe."

I think that last part was aimed more at Rake to ensure his good behavior than for Dr. Carey's peace of mind.

"That my home was taken from Regor indicates there's great trouble in our capital," Rake said. "That trouble seems to be spreading here. We need answers now. Have you been able to contact Tam?" he asked Gethen.

"No, sir, I have not." Gethen paused uneasily. "It is even more critical now that we reach him."

Rake went still. "How so?"

"Buried in the rubble near the center of the house was a crystal, its interior burning with tongues of flame."

Now I got to hear Rake repeat Gethen's go-to word.

"We're not doing this again," Ian warned. "First Gethen recognized the rock, now you. He wouldn't tell us anything until he reported to you. I accepted that. He's reported it. That thing's in our lab. We need to know what we brought home."

Gethen answered for his boss. "As I said, Agent Byrne, if it is what I believe, it is not dangerous in its present state. The containment box your lab is using will be more than sufficient."

"That doesn't answer my question."

"And I am not the one to answer it for you," Rake told him. "I know next to nothing about these crystals."

"You know enough to know they're dangerous."

Gethen had cryptically requested that the lab maintain full containment on its newest guest. He'd told them there was an expert Rake would contact who would be able to tell them more about it.

"Is your cousin Tam the crystal expert?" I asked Rake.

"He's the closest to one I know of. As chancellor to the goblin king and queen, he also knows everything that happens in Regor."

"Around the crystal was what looked like melted metal," I said. "Roughly the size of a wheeled carry-on bag."

"Tulis told me what happened," Rake said. "Two Khrynsani were seen breaking the wards and entering the back of the house carrying what looked to be a small chest. They left less than ten minutes later—without the chest. The witness reported the incident to the city watch, who alerted Tulis, who was with my parents at their house outside of Regor. Tulis arrived that night and searched the house. He found the chest in a storage closet in my study. Something in the chest was humming and glowing. He felt dizzy and disoriented as the walls started to fade, then his body did the same. He's not sure if he lost consciousness at that point, or even briefly ceased to exist. His next awareness was intense pressure as his body again solidified, as did the house around him. He said the heat from the chest was like standing in front of an open furnace. A Khrynsani ran into the room and was surprised to see Tulis there. They fought. The fire started when the floor under the chest caught fire. Tulis killed the Khrynsani and forced his soul into his lifestone. He admits that he was then overcome with weakness from whatever had happened to him and from the smoke. Then he woke up here."

When Rake finished Tulis's story he was met with a whole lot of silence. I knew I'd have plenty of questions once my brain caught up with what my ears had just heard. As it stood, I had only one thing to say.

"Wow."

"It sounds like the Khrynsani's body we found may have come from here," Ian said, "meaning our world."

Rake nodded. "Tulis said that he was strangely garbed. From what he described, it sounded like jeans, T-shirt, and a leather jacket."

"He came to retrieve the device?" I wondered out loud. "I imagine if all they wanted to bring here was the house, their agent finding Tulis inside was a huge shock."

Rake's eyes glittered dangerously. "Knowing Tulis, the

Khrynsani didn't live long enough to be shocked. We will find out from him soon enough."

Gethen pushed Tulis's wheelchair with Rake by his side. Dr. Carey wanted Tulis back in bed. The goblin mage wanted to see the rock that had brought him here.

We didn't know if it had been teleportation or something like it, but there was no disputing that Rake's house with Tulis inside had been in Regor, and then it had appeared in New York. Even if it wasn't teleportation, that's what we were gonna call it until a better explanation came along.

SPI's lab mages had contained the crystal to the best of their ability, considering how little they knew about it.

So, we were all safe being in the same room with it. Unless we weren't.

The inorganics lab was on one side of the hall, organics on the other. Both were equipped to handle, contain, and analyze virtually anything. The dead Khrynsani's body had been taken to the organics side of the hall where Bert Ferguson's workroom was located. We entered the inorganics lab. Though after what the crystal had done and the creepy impression I'd gotten from it, I wasn't sure it'd been brought to the right place.

Floor-to-ceiling glass along both sides of the hall provided an unobstructed view into both labs. It wasn't glass, but it was shatterproof, explosion proof, and every other proof the headquarters' builders could come up with. That way, if an experiment or subject got out of control, those windows served two purposes: Keep the chaos in the lab, and let the folks in the lab across the hall know that all hell had broken loose and to call for help.

There was never a dull moment at SPI.

We went into an observation room adjacent to the containment area where the lab techs had secured the crystal.

The cause of all the trouble was about the size of a jagged softball.

It had been smug when Gethen had plucked it out of the smoking rubble, and now it appeared to be happy as an innocent clam in its new home of a clear, blast- and magic-proof cube. Whether the rock felt warm and fuzzy wasn't the point; whether we felt safe from it was. Anything that could do what it did was as dangerous as a live nuke, and our lab people were treating it accordingly.

It wasn't the only rock presently in SPI custody. On the other side of the inorganics lab in another ultra-secure testing area was the magetech generator, created by an interdimensional supervillain, that had taken the Regor Regency Hotel and its hundreds of guests into our own little pocket dimension of horrors. The power source for the generator was a fist-sized glowing blue cube. Ian had stabbed the cube with his ancestor's spear to stop the countdown that would have resulted in… Well, since it hadn't happened, we didn't know exactly what the result would have been, but we were pretty sure none of us would've survived.

Just last week our lab geniuses had determined enough about the magetech generator to be pretty sure that it'd be safe for Ian to pull the spear from the stone, so to speak. He did, and the generator didn't—blow us up, that is. It still had its own dedicated team of technicians working to determine how the generator had been built, how it worked, and what its full capabilities were.

Ian hadn't said anything during the time he'd spent without his spear, but I knew he'd missed it. At first, I'd been ambivalent about my partner's new quasi-partner. It'd been made by the master craftsmen of the Tuatha dé Danann, an ancient race of Irish gods. We'd found out a couple of months ago that Ian was the direct descendant of Lugh Lámhfhada, a legendary warrior/demigod. Ian now carried the spear that'd saved our collective bacon as a proud part of his daily arsenal. Our armorers had outfitted it with a telescoping shaft so that it would fit comfortably in its custom harness against Ian's spine and under any jacket he wore.

I think I'd missed having that spear with us almost as much as Ian had.

Tulis took a good look at the flickering crystal, shook his head, and said a few words.

"He hasn't seen it before," Rake translated. "I almost wish I could say the same. I've never seen one, but I have heard of it—and others like it. Gethen, I believe you're right."

"Others?" I asked.

In our little slice of the lab, you could've heard a pin drop.

"And now you're going to tell the rest of us what Gethen was right about," Ian said. "Correct?" From the tone of my partner's voice, it was clearly a rhetorical question. Rake would tell us what was going on, or the folks in the organics lab across the hall would be calling in a security emergency.

Rake turned to Gethen. "Do you have Padiri *constantly* trying to reach Tam?"

"Yes. And I've told her to contact Imala Kalis if she can't reach him."

Rake stood there, never taking his eyes from the flickering stone.

Ian cleared his throat. "Rake," he growled in warning.

Rake blew out his breath. "My cousin Tamnais Nathrach recently led an expedition to an uninhabited continent on our world. It was once home to an ancient goblin civilization. Legend said they used 'crystals of flame' to power their city—lights, pumps for a water system, heating and cooling, everything."

"Sheesh, it *does* sound nuclear," I muttered.

"When he and his team arrived," Rake continued, "the Khrynsani had gotten there first."

"And started a rock collection," Ian surmised.

Rake nodded. "It does appear that way, though intergalactic teleportation was not on the list of the crystals' capabilities. That this one was in the hands of the Khrynsani, *and* that they were able to somehow use it to bring my house here…"

Someone in a white lab coat stepped up beside me.

It was Ben Sadler—now Dr. Ben Sadler. Curly blond hair, blue eyes, in his twenties and still didn't look old enough to shave. He was SPI's new consulting gem mage. He was also a Level Ten, the tip top of the talent pool.

In his pre-SPI life of only a year ago, Ben had been a diamond appraiser at Christie's. After an incident involving seven cursed diamonds, three harpy jewel thieves, and one Russian dragon/oligarch, Ben had been identified as a rogue talent—untrained, untested, and unpredictable, dangerous to himself and everyone else.

Aside from that, Ben was just a sweet guy who occasionally made questionable life choices, like tangling with harpies in the midst of a diamond heist.

Ben stood on tiptoe to see over Rake's shoulder at what all the hubbub was about.

He blanched. "*Another* one?"

I froze. "You mean another rock, like the cube over there, right?"

Ben pointed at the flickering crystal. "No, I mean another one, *just like that*."

7

SPI's job was dealing with the unexpected, but some things were more unexpected than others.

"It came in an hour ago," Ben told us as we followed him to the middle of the lab to where the twin to our recent acquisition waited, sealed in its own protective observation box.

"We" included Ian, Rake, and myself. Dr. Carey had taken charge of Tulis, and Gethen had stepped out of the lab to make a few calls. Thanks to the glass walls, Gethen was able to have privacy for his calls, and make good on his vow not to let Rake out of his sight.

"We only have the basics of the report," Ben continued, "enough to know it needs to be in a containment case until we find out more. It was found on a newly empty plot of land outside Sawpit, Colorado. Newly empty, meaning an old lumber mill had been there the last time anyone looked."

"Sounds like our softball from outer space," I noted, "only in reverse."

Rake gave Ben the condensed version of our past twelve hours.

"Where's Sawpit?" I asked Ben when Rake finished.

"Northwest of Telluride. Population of less than fifty. The mill hasn't been operational since the 1950s. We got lucky. The couple who noticed the mill being gone are clued in to the supernatural. On weekends, they like to photograph abandoned buildings. The first weekend they went, the mill was there. The next weekend it was gone, even the foundation, nothing left except the ground underneath." Ben stopped in front of a case identical to the one we'd just left. "And this little guy."

Our cosmic softball had a galactic golf ball friend.

When Ben referred to it, I could swear its flickers turned coyly flirtatious.

"That rock wants you to pick it up," I muttered.

Ben stayed put. "Yeah, we've decided I shouldn't do that quite yet."

"Wise choice."

"The couple called a friend of theirs who works in our Denver office," Ben continued. "They sent a team to investigate, and the first thing our people did was pack up this crystal and send it here for study."

While SPI had offices worldwide, our New York lab had the fanciest gizmos and gadgets for finding out what made supernatural stuff tick—without blowing everyone up in the process.

"What have you determined so far?" Rake asked him.

"That we're way out of our league."

While Rake wanted to question the dead Khrynsani now, finding out as much as we could about what we were dealing with would go a long way toward asking the right questions. As we'd experienced with the soul of Alastor Malvolia—aka the dead goblin lawyer baked in the cookie oven—you had one chance and limited time to question a disembodied soul. You needed to ask the right questions quickly because once that soul began to fade, you weren't going to get a second chance.

We finally got some good news. One of Gethen's calls had been to Padiri, who'd been charged with contacting Rake's cousin. She'd finally gotten through, and Cousin Tam would be paying us a visit as soon as he could finalize arrangements on his end.

Rake had told me that the goblin king and queen had not only elevated Tam to chancellor, they'd appointed him their heir until they produced one of their own. Like Rake, Tam was a dark mage and closely involved with the goblin intelligence service. To me, it sounded like Tam and Rake were two branches of the same inscrutable tree. I wondered if Ian would feel an urge to punch Tam, too.

That was another reason for holding off on the questioning—Rake wanted Tam to be here. He might know this particular Khrynsani, which could be a huge help.

The softball had been collected two hours ago. The golf ball had been found early this morning and flown directly to New York on one of Vivienne Sagadraco's private jets. Strange things from all over the world were sent to our headquarters' labs all the time; on our world, that added up to a lot of weirdness. It might have taken another hour or two, but it would have been noted that the lab had two of the same kind of crystal from two different locations. Thanks to Ben Sadler's curiosity, the math had gotten done a little faster.

Now, we were in Ms. Sagadraco's office suite overlooking SPI's agent bullpen. The boss had a private conference room adjacent to her office. That's where we'd gathered. Dr. Claire Cheban, SPI's lab director, had joined us, as had Kenji Hayashi and Alain Moreau.

The boss had arranged for a teleconference from the site of the building disappearance in Sawpit.

To my surprise, Kitty Poertner's face appeared on the screen. It looked like somebody had been called in from vacation.

Kitty's family lived near Casper, Wyoming. Last week, she'd taken Yasha out to meet her folks. Luckily for us she was only one state north of Sawpit.

While Kitty could see all of us seated around the table, she zeroed in on me first. "Sorry we missed your party."

"No worries," I said quickly. "Yasha meeting your folks was more important."

Especially when the new man in your life was a werewolf.

I didn't ask how the meeting had gone. After all, the big boss was sitting right here. I was sure it hadn't been completely uneventful, but since Kitty and I were besties, she'd tell me all the awkwardness later. I couldn't see Yasha, but I also couldn't see Kitty leaving him with her parents. He was there somewhere.

I took a sharp left back toward business. "And it looks like you were in the right place at the right time to help us out."

Kitty was another of SPI's consultants. Her day job was owning and running a bakery on Bleecker Street in the Village, but her family came from a long line of portalkeepers. They could open, close, detect, and destroy them. Kitty was one of the best.

"What do you have for us, Ms. Poertner?" Ms. Sagadraco asked. "I realize a building disappearing doesn't meet the usual criteria for a portal, but are we dealing with a portal-like phenomenon?"

"Not in any sense I've ever encountered. Thanks to the couple who reported it, we're able to say the disappearance happened more than eight days ago. Unfortunately, that's long enough for most magic signatures to have faded. Most, but not all. We've detected magic, and a technology we only refer to as alien because we have never seen anything like it." Kitty glanced back over her shoulder. Occasionally while she spoke, we could see people moving back and forth behind her. I assumed they were our Denver lab team. "Carter Bates— he's in charge of the local team—could explain the technology angle better, and he should be available in a few minutes. As to a more mundane explanation, there was no sign that the building had been destroyed or taken apart and hauled away. In fact, the only tire tracks were from the Sawyers' ATV from last weekend and this one. That's Chuck and Didi Sawyer. They're the ones who found and reported it. No one else has been up here in the time in between. It was as if the sawmill was lifted right off its foundation."

Ms. Sagadraco arched a silvery eyebrow. "Lifted?"

"Dr. Bates says that's apparently what happened. Like a big hand reached down and scooped it up."

"Could it have been vaporized?" Dr. Cheban asked.

Claire Cheban didn't look old enough to be out of college, let alone have a PhD and be in charge of a lab like SPI's. That she was in charge and had not one, but two hard science doctorates, said all that needed to be said about SPI's chief scientist. That she had asked if an entire building had been vaporized said everything about what SPI dealt with on a daily basis. Yes, it was possible. It would be classified as magic, but it was possible.

Kitty shook her head. "There was no sign that heat of any kind had been involved. No scorched earth or signs of a fire. The Sawyers thought it was bizarre enough that the building was gone, but then they found the crystal. They'd never seen anything like it. That's when they called their friend in Denver. While the crystal may not have had anything to do with the building's disappearance—"

"We believe it did," Ms. Sagadraco said. "Lord Danescu, if you would, please."

Rake told Kitty what had happened.

Kitty just stood there for a few blinks. "Wow."

I snorted. "Yeah, that's what I said."

Coming from a woman who had single-handedly collapsed and sealed a gate to Hell to prevent Earth from being overrun by a demonic invasion, that "wow" carried a lot of weight.

Kitty glanced off to the side. "Dr. Bates is available now. I'll turn you over to him."

The man who took Kitty's place in our screen had short dark hair and wore black-rimmed glasses on a narrow face. He appeared to be in his mid-forties.

"Director Sagadraco, my apologies for not being able to speak with you sooner."

"No apologies needed, Agent Bates. Did you hear Lord Danescu's account of what has happened here?"

"I did, and I share Ms. Poertner's opinion. Impressive."

Ms. Sagadraco scanned through a document on her tablet with her index finger. "I asked Agent Hayashi to join us because he's just completed his report on the incident here."

Dr. Bates grinned. "I have to say I'm jealous, Kenji."

"We saw the end of it, not the during, unfortunately," Kenji told him. "And we didn't get visuals from any of our surveillance cameras. We've covered the entire Washington Square Park area, including the Full Moon. We picked up the flame-colored lightshow above the vacant lot, but at the instant before the building appeared, every camera we had stopped working. It was probably about the same time the lights went out and our phones died. How are your electronics doing there?"

"No problems, though we have detected higher than normal levels of electromagnetic radiation."

That didn't sound good. "Do you mean like when a nuclear bomb goes off and anything electronic gets fried?"

"Not to that level, Agent Fraser," Dr. Bates assured me. "Electromagnetic radiation is produced by medical equipment such as X-ray machines and ultrasounds, down to microwave ovens, laptops, and cell phones. By higher than normal levels, I was referring to how unusual it is to detect any EMR out here, let alone to the level of…say a medical research facility."

"Were there any reports in the past week of an unexplained power outage?" Kenji asked.

"Let me check. The local sheriff's here. He's a werewolf,

which has been invaluable for keeping a lid on all this." Dr. Bates stepped away from the camera, returning a few minutes later.

"That's an affirmative, Kenji. Five nights ago, there was what sounded like a muted explosion and all electronics stopped working for nearly two hours, from Sawpit down to Telluride. It was a clear night with no storms in the area."

"Then that's when your sawmill vanished," Kenji told him.

There was a knock at the door, and Mr. Moreau went to answer it, then slipped outside, closing the door behind him.

He was back in less than thirty seconds, his expression grim.

"We've had five more building disappearances."

8

In the past hour, two incidents had grown to seven. Seven buildings vanished without a trace. Well, six disappearances and one rather spectacular appearance.

That we knew about.

I was sure there were going to be more. When talented bad guys got rolling, there were always more.

Crystals hadn't been found at those additional five sites. Yet.

Vivienne Sagadraco issued orders to Kenji and Mr. Moreau. Kenji was to contact all SPI offices worldwide, tell them what we had here, and see if they'd encountered more of the same. The additional disappearances had all been in the US, but the boss wanted a complete picture of the problem. And oh boy, was it a problem. Entire buildings going bye-bye wasn't what you'd call subtle. People would notice. People with smartphones and cameras. Ms. Sagadraco got Kylie to work monitoring news and social media for any mention of building-related strangeness and to report any findings to Mr. Moreau and Kenji. Mr. Moreau would center his attentions on the mortal authorities.

The boss lady was going with us.

"Us" consisted of Rake, myself, Ian, and Gethen—and the goblin assassin's soul trapped in the pendant inside Gethen's pocket, which I was doing my best not to think about.

We were going to Rake's apartment to meet his cousin Tamnais Nathrach.

Two cases that we knew of involved a crystal not from our world, but likely from Rake and Tam's. According to Rake, Tam had had first-hand experience with the motherlode where the two crystals in our lab had come from.

We needed answers. Now.

Dragons were big on protocol, and Tam was chancellor and heir (albeit temporary) to the goblin monarchs. Protocol dictated that Ms. Sagadraco be there to greet him, but practicality demanded it. Tam Nathrach was an expert on the alien crystals and the Khrynsani brotherhood likely responsible for planting at least one of them. Somehow, I couldn't see a cadre of evil, Nazi-like goblins running amuck in New York and Colorado, but hey, stranger things have happened.

Vivienne Sagadraco lived at the same Central Park West address as Rake. He owned many properties in New York, and their apartment building was one of them. Though to be exact, he was only half owner. Ms. Sagadraco had owned the other half since it'd been built, and Rake had bought out her partner when he was ready to sell and go home. I'd always kind of wondered where "home" was. Having met a few of Ms. Sagadraco's friends, I suspected her former partner's home wasn't on our world or even in our dimension.

Over the past few months since Rake and I had become serious, I'd been a regular visitor to the building. Rake had given me a key, though I'd never used it. I still maintained my own apartment, and had only been to Rake's place when he'd been there. Regardless, Rake had made sure that I was welcomed by his staff whenever I visited, from the building's doormen to his butler, housekeeper, and cook. Once they'd gotten to know me, all had said they were glad that Rake was seeing me, and they felt that I was a good influence on him.

Since the press had been camped out in front of Rake's building since last night, the SPI driver took the agency SUV to the private parking garage entrance.

Rake's penthouse apartment looked like something out of *Architectural Digest.* Artsy, yet tasteful. Comfortable, but not cozy. Rake didn't do cozy, and he didn't entertain at home. He considered his home his personal refuge. Period. Any and all business was conducted elsewhere. Having an elsewhere at your disposal wasn't a problem when you owned properties throughout the city, including a five-star hotel that catered specifically to the supernatural one percent.

On the drive over, Rake had alerted his staff to expect us. After a perfunctory offer of refreshments, which we politely refused, they left us to our business.

At the center of Rake's apartment was a midsized room set aside for his magical workings. It was accessible only to Rake and Gethen—by a locking system both mechanical and magical—and to the goblin who awaited us inside.

Berat Tane was the new portal mage at Rake's Regor

Regency Hotel, replacing Kenan Chaitan, who had been killed recently defending the hotel's portal from both elven and goblin terrorists.

In addition to portals, Berat could operate a mirror.

Rake's mirror, with its sturdy metal frame, was nearly seven feet tall and three feet wide. It wasn't a mirror to admire yourself in. It was for transport. Mirror mages could connect two specially constructed mirrors, enabling a person to step into the mirror on their end, and step out of the destination mirror. Distances in miles or between worlds could be covered in a single step.

That was the extent of my knowledge of how this thing worked, and I was pretty sure I didn't want to receive enlightenment on what went on in between. Rake had mentioned that last year there'd been a bit of a giant spider infestation in the Void, which was what the space between mirrors was called.

Nope and nope.

I didn't need to know anything else, since Satan would be serving snow cones in Hell before I'd ever step through one.

Rake's portal mage stood about five feet in front of the mirror, one arm extended, palm out, fingers spread wide, his stance one of casual readiness.

"My lord, Chancellor Nathrach's mage has activated the mirror on their end and is ready when we are."

Rake nodded once. "Bring him through."

The mage straightened his stance, facing the mirror, now with both arms extended toward a surface that began to ripple, then swirl, picking up speed.

I quickly looked down at my feet. There wasn't enough Dramamine in the world for me to be able to look at an activated mirror and not lose lunch. I'd seen one before and had looked at the pretty, swirly colors a little too long. A pulsing light reflected on the polished floor, and then thankfully, the light show stopped.

I looked up at the new arrival.

Chancellor Tamnais Nathrach wore black, and he wore it well. Rake's cousin was leather armored from his torso down to the toes of his over-the-knee boots. He was wearing blades everywhere there was room. He also had what looked like a dark canvas gym bag slung over one shoulder.

Yes, the view was nice; but I think what dropped my jaw was that Tam Nathrach could have been Rake's nearly twin brother. The only big difference was that Rake's hair was shoulder length, and Tam wore his to the middle of his back.

Rake gave his cousin a quick up-and-down glance and grinned. "Expecting trouble?"

Tam responded with a crooked grin of his own. "Forever and always."

The two men hugged, Rake being careful to maneuver around his cousin's portable arsenal.

No, this wasn't gonna be awkward in any way, shape, or form.

Rake handled the introductions.

When Tam took my hand, I noticed the ring on the hand clasping mine.

A ring set with a stone that had tiny, flickering flames inside.

The band was the twisted, golden body of a dragon. Its four claws gripped the stone, with its mouth open as if breathing fire into it.

Yikes.

Tam released my hand and held up his to display the ring. "Is this what you've found?"

"Times two and both bigger." Rake indicated the door. "Why don't we make ourselves comfortable while you tell us just how much trouble we're in."

Once we were back in the living room with its floor-to-ceiling windows, Tam stopped and gazed out over the expansive view of Central Park. No wide eyes, no tenseness, no signs of an impending freak-out at being dozens of stories above the ground. This was not the reaction of a man who had never seen any building over four stories high.

I stepped up beside him. "I take it you've been here before."

Tam's dark eyes never left the view. "More than once, and it never ceases to mesmerize, especially at night."

"It's going to be a long day," Rake told his cousin. "And we have a dead Khrynsani to interrogate. Have you eaten?"

"It's been a few hours."

Rake nodded. "I'll have Saralle put together a light lunch."

"And I should probably change into something more appropriate for where we're going."

Rake gestured down the hall toward the bedrooms. "As always, everything is ready for you."

Tam gave Ms. Sagadraco and me a little bow. "If you will excuse me, I won't be long." With that, he strode down the hall, disappearing from view.

We all waited until the bedroom door had closed behind him.

Ms. Sagadraco was wearing an amused little smile. "A remarkable resemblance, Lord Danescu."

"Good, it's not just me," Ian muttered. "Did you know he'd be wearing one of those rocks like a mood ring?"

"That took me by surprise," Rake admitted. "Perhaps they're only dangerous under certain conditions, or at a specific size."

Tam reemerged about ten minutes later in a dark, perfectly tailored suit, similar to the many bespoke suits in Rake's closet. His hair was still loose, though now tucked behind his pointed ears. "Looks like Rake took you shopping on a previous visit here," I noted.

Tam smiled. "I've found it takes a lot to attract undue attention in this city, but it's better to err on the side of caution."

Rake's staff served their idea of a light lunch on the large coffee table. The trays of sandwiches would've fed an army—or at least one of our commando units. Rake was right; we needed to eat while we could, and eating gave my hands something to do while my eyes kept darting to Tam's ring. I couldn't help but think of it as an itty-bitty nuclear warhead.

Tam noticed. "I promise, the ring is harmless."

Ian set his empty plate aside. Coming from a military and then police background, Ian not only ate when he could, he could eat quickly. "I wish I could say the same for the two in our lab. What are they?"

Rake pulled out his phone and showed Tam the photos Gethen had taken at the site of the fire. "Is it one of the Nidaar crystals?"

Tam looked and scowled. "Undoubtedly. How large are they?"

I started to say "softball" and "golf ball," but stopped

myself. Tam's Earth education might not have extended that far.

Rake used his hands to show the approximate sizes.

"And a crystal that small somehow brought your house in Regor *here*?" Tam asked incredulously.

Ms. Sagadraco set her teacup and saucer aside. "Exactly what are we dealing with, Chancellor Nathrach?"

"Until last year, we believed the Heart of Nidaar to be a legend." Tam was a fast eater, too. He set his now empty plate on the coffee table. "It's a harsh environment, so only the coasts of Aquas—that's the name of the continent—have ever been explored. In ancient times, it was said to have been inhabited by our distant cousins. We have silver skin and black hair, whereas the Cha'Nidaar were golden-skinned and white-haired. They were said to live in a great city beneath a mountain with a stone that could command the power of the land and seas." Tam settled back on the sofa. "We found out it's not a legend. The stone, the city, the people—they're all real. Nine hundred years ago, a group of Khrynsani found the city. They used black magic to defeat the city's guards and reach the Heart of Nidaar, the motherstone. The Khrynsani's clumsy attempts to activate and test the stone's capabilities caused a series of earthquakes that destroyed thousands of miles of Aquas's eastern coast, drained every lake and river, and turned a green paradise into a barren wasteland."

Tam leaned forward, elbows on his knees. "Subsequent expeditions searched for the city, but couldn't find any trace of Nidaar or its people. It was believed that they perished in the quakes. Then last year, a Khrynsani expedition again found the mountain range containing the city and its people. They had intentionally hidden themselves to protect the Heart of

Nidaar and prevent what had happened from ever happening again. For the safety of the Seven Kingdoms, this time we had to reach the Heart of Nidaar first."

"And two pieces of that thing is what we have in our lab?" Ian asked.

Tam nodded. "Two exceedingly small pieces. The actual Heart of Nidaar fills an entire cavern in the center of a mountain. Veins of the crystals run deep, which explains how it can cause earthquakes."

"It's a long way from earthquakes to plucking a building off the face of the earth," Ian said. "Or dropping one from your world onto a vacant lot here."

"The Cha'Nidaar have guarded the Heart of Nidaar for thousands of years and know everything it's capable of," Tam said. "That ability isn't one of them."

"Then how?"

"I can't explain."

Gethen spoke for the first time in quite a while. "What did the Khrynsani want it for?"

"To power portals and gates to take the Khrynsani and their Sythsaurian invader allies anywhere in the Seven Kingdoms. They could put assassins into palaces, armies inside cities— and we would be powerless to predict where and when they would strike. We thought the crystals would be rare, but the city and mountain were filled with them. Since the Khrynsani arrived before we did, they had ample opportunity to gather as many as they wanted."

"Back up, cousin," Rake said. "Sythsaurian *invaders*?"

"I forget you haven't been home in a while." Tam barked a humorless laugh. "A lot has happened."

"Obviously. Care to bring me up to speed?"

"The Khrynsani have allied themselves with an alien race to conquer our world. Though 'conquer' is a misnomer. The Sythsaurians want to enslave or consume every living creature and resource they can use, and when our world is a lifeless shell, they'll move on to the next world suitable for feeding."

Rake was aghast. "How the hell could you forget to tell me *that*?"

Tam gave his cousin a flat stare. "I've been a little busy."

Ms. Sagadraco spoke. "Please continue, Chancellor Nathrach."

"We encountered Sythsaurians in Nidaar, but they have yet to put in an appearance in the Seven Kingdoms. Six of the seven kingdoms recently signed an alliance to share any intelligence and combine our armies to meet the Sythsaurians and the Khrynsani when, or if, an invasion comes to pass."

"Who's the holdout?" Rake asked.

"Nebia."

Rake snorted derisively. "Figures."

"We're better off without them," Tam said. "Though there'll be the annoyance of having to watch our backs."

"The Khrynsani know about our world," Ian said. "If these Sythsaurians invade your world with their help, what is to stop them from invading ours?"

"Us, Agent Byrne." Ms. Sagadraco poured herself another cup of tea. "*We* will do everything in our power to stop them. If this does happen, it would become necessary to tell the appropriate agencies on this world what we are facing. In fact, I have contacts in those agencies, and would very much like to brief them on the potential threat." She looked to Tam. "I will gather my senior staff this afternoon. Chancellor Nathrach, once you view the crystals at headquarters, I would very much appreciate you telling us all that you know."

Tam inclined his head. "I will gladly do so, madam."

The boss glanced around at us. "First, we must eliminate the threat we presently face. Chancellor Nathrach, it is obvious that you survived the expedition to Nidaar. How did you dispose of this cavern-sized crystal?"

"The ruler of the Cha'Nidaar acknowledged that it had become too great a risk to allow *anyone* access to the Heart of Nidaar. Since it couldn't be destroyed, she ordered the city evacuated, and we worked with her engineers to destroy the city and the mountain above it. The Heart of Nidaar is buried under them both."

"That's some demolition," Ian said with something akin to admiration.

Tam flashed a crooked grin. "We had a lot of talented and enthusiastic help." He turned to Gethen. "I understand you have the lifestone from the Khrynsani agent."

"I do."

"May I see it, please? There's a chance I may know him personally."

I raised an eyebrow. "You might know him? Aren't the Khrynsani…evil?"

"They are. But until recently, the Khrynsani all but ruled our land, and their leader was nearly crowned king." Tam's dark eyes glittered. "I'm a firm believer in knowing my enemies very well."

Gethen held the pendant by its chain, and Tam carefully took it from him, raising the pendant to dangle mere inches away from his eyes. He smiled slowly, exposing the tips of his fangs. "Khent Mendiu, Sandrina Ghalfari's favorite errand boy. Ladies and gentlemen, we are about to get some answers."

"Who's Sandrina Ghalfari?" I asked.

"Her son was the head of the Khrynsani until his supposed death," Tam replied. "Then she took over."

"*Supposed* death?"

Tam grinned in a flash of fangs. "Turns out being carried off screaming by a giant demon into the Lower Hells isn't as fatal as one would think. I was very disappointed. I went to a lot of trouble to conjure that demon."

9

We'd managed to sneak into Rake's building, but to leave, we'd have to walk out the front door.

Through a gauntlet of press and paparazzi.

The local newshounds hadn't given up on Rake. A notorious billionaire had carried a man out of a burning building on his previously vacant lot, and then disappeared with the victim.

It went beyond irresistible. Reporters had to find out what happened, and the social media addicts had to know. That neither group was getting any information just increased the frenzy to get their hands on it.

The only SUV available at headquarters hadn't had a full tank of gas. While we were inside, our driver had gone to fill up. When he returned, the street outside the underground garage entrance was blocked by a broken-down garbage truck.

Time for some disguises.

Ms. Sagadraco wore her usual human form. The press knew her as a wealthy socialite and generous philanthropist who lived in the building. Fortunately, Ian and I still had our amulets from this morning, and with Rake's help, we activated them again. Rake, Gethen, and Tam came up with their own glamours.

Ian and Gethen looked like bodyguards, so they went with that. Ms. Sagadraco's bodyguards. I tagged along behind like a personal assistant.

In their suits, Tam and Rake looked like a pair of Wall Streeters on their way to work with duffel bags to hit the gym after. Gorgeous Wall Streeters. I had no idea who the press thought they were, in relation to Ms. Sagadraco. Stockbroker boy toys?

Rake's usual glamour merely altered the aspects of his appearance that would be most alarming to our average human on the street. Fangs were blunted, ear tips rounded, and gray skin changed to a heathy human tan. That's what the press would be looking for, so Rake had to do a little more work this time. Tam pretty much copied what Rake had done, so they ended up looking like brothers.

In hindsight, they probably should have altered their hair.

Our SPI driver was waiting in front of the building. It was late afternoon and traffic was gearing up for the evening rush. Foot traffic had picked up, too. It was also a breezy day, so when Rake and Tam set foot outside, a gust of wind swept their hair to the side and collisions occurred, on and off the street. Tam looked like he was starring in a Pantene commercial.

Cameras started clicking. I don't think the paparazzi could help themselves.

Ian helped Ms. Sagadraco into the back of the SUV, and the rest of us piled in as quickly as we could.

Ian took the front passenger seat. He always had shotgun when we went out, because more than once, an actual shotgun had been needed. Yasha kept one under the driver's seat and the front passenger seat. I didn't know if that was a Yasha thing or agency policy, because I rarely rode with anyone except Yasha.

I missed him. Not the hair-raising, near-suicidal dashes through New York's streets, but our big, lovable werewolf partner. I hoped he and Kitty could wrap things up in Colorado and come home soon.

Ms. Sagadraco's driver pulled smoothly out into traffic without any of us having a near-death experience. I had to admit it was nice.

Tam looked out the window as we made our way down Central Park West toward SPI headquarters.

I had to ask. "Even though you've been here before, how strange is this to you?"

"I think of automobiles as horseless carriages, which is what I believe they were once called, though these are much more comfortable and quiet. You can actually carry on a conversation, and the ride is infinitely smoother."

I could see Ian in profile from the front seat. He was grinning. "That depends on who's driving."

Looked like I wasn't the only one to miss Yasha, but not his driving.

Then the grin vanished, and my partner was all business. "How much experience have you had with these crystals?"

"More than I would like, but less than I believe you'll need."

Ian's frown deepened. "Is it going to be enough?"

"There are two undisputed experts," Tam said. "One is unable to travel due to her age and health. The other is out of reach, though I have people trying to try to contact her. She is our world's top gem mage."

Tam proceeded to tell us about Baeseria, the queen of the Cha'Nidaar, and Agata Azul, the aforementioned best gem mage his world had to offer.

"Agata wears a shard of the Heart of Nidaar similar to mine, except hers is in a pendant. Her bond with it guided us to the city of Nidaar. She and Baeseria calmed the Heart of Nidaar itself, preventing it from destroying our world."

"What does your ring do?" Ian asked.

"It would be capable of the same as Agata's pendant, if I had her gift, which I don't." As Tam regarded the ring, it flickered almost cheerfully. "Both were given to my ancestor by the Cha'Nidaar queen. I wear it to remind me of what he suffered at the hands of the Khrynsani."

The best we had was Ben Sadler, who'd said this morning that we were way out of our league.

"You're trying *really* hard to find Agata, right?" I asked.

"I am, but she's on what I believe you would call a top-secret mission, and we have been unable to contact her, or my two friends who are with her."

"Who?" Rake asked.

"Raine and Mychael. I've spoken with Justinius Valerian. He's attempting to reach them as well. But for now, I'm afraid we're on our own."

Rake and Tam dropped their glamours and attracted a similar level of attention—minus the fender benders—once we were inside SPI headquarters, though there were two minor personnel collisions resulting in a nearly dropped laptop and flying paperwork.

If the two goblins noticed the impression they made, they gave no sign.

Ms. Sagadraco led the way to the lab where our unwanted guests waited.

Tam approached the larger of the two crystals, and I could swear the closer Tam got, the happier the crystal seemed. Its flickering turned downright excited. The smaller one flickered even faster, as if vying for his attentions. Tam's ring pulsed in response.

"That's interesting," he noted.

Ben walked up. "They seem to like me, too. Considering what they're capable of, the feeling isn't mutual."

"I take it you haven't touched them yet?" I asked.

"Not until I get to know them better, and maybe not even then."

Vivienne Sagadraco did the honors. "Chancellor Nathrach, this is Dr. Ben Sadler, a gem mage who consults for us when we have need. Dr. Sadler, Tamnais Nathrach comes to us from Governor Danescu's home world to help resolve our present difficulty."

"I don't know how much help I can be with these crystals," Tam said, shaking Ben's hand, "but I will do everything I can. I'm afraid my skills are in other areas."

Ben's smile was more of a frozen rictus. "I've heard you're here to question the…er, arson suspect."

Apparently, I wasn't the only one a little freaked out that Tam and Rake were about to interrogate a dead guy. I was pretty sure I could work at SPI for decades and not get used to that.

"Yes, but Rake and I wanted to stop here first," Tam told him. "We will have limited time with the Khrynsani's soul. It's vital to know as much as possible going in, so we can better focus our questioning."

I was all for changing the subject from talking to dead people. "Ben, you're saying that the crystal *is* alive in some way?"

"Life goes far beyond our human experience," Dr. Cheban replied from nearby. As she approached us, her eyes flicked left to Rake, then right to Tam, noting the likeness—in an entirely scientific way, of course.

"We're cousins," Rake said before she could ask.

"Fascinating."

Yes, it was. And every female in the lab and some of the males were in total agreement.

She extended her hand to Tam. "Claire Cheban, director of the labs here at SPI." She smiled. "I take it you are our eagerly awaited crystal expert?"

Tam took her hand and bowed over it. "I don't know if I would go that far," he said, returning her smile. "I can provide some insight about what you have, but as to how it was used to bring a house here from our world, I'm afraid I'm at a loss."

"We hope to be able to answer that one ourselves. We're analyzing the metallic residue found around it in the rubble."

"You've determined that it is a metal then?" Ms. Sagadraco asked.

"At least partially. It's steel and an element we haven't been able to identify. We suspect it will be alien in composition."

"Alien as in not from our world?" Ian asked.

"Correct. The same is true of the cube. Less than half of the elements we detected in the cube are found on our world." Claire indicated the crystal. "Unlike this specimen, the cube is a manufactured power cell."

"Have you determined how it was made?" Ms. Sagadraco asked.

"We suspect the process was similar to manufacturing synthetic diamonds, involving high pressure and temperature. The presses for making diamonds weigh hundreds of tons and must withstand temperatures upward of fourteen hundred degrees centigrade. The process takes up to three months for diamonds of only a few carats. If the cube were to be assigned a carat weight, it would be approximately five thousand."

Rake whistled. "So, it's a kind of diamond?"

Ben took that question. "Not any that I can identify, either through conventional or unconventional means."

We all knew what Ben meant by "unconventional." He'd actually touched the cube and had deemed it to be so alien as to not qualify as a gem.

"One of our mages determined that there was complex magic involved as well," Claire added.

"If it is time-consuming and expensive to produce," Ms. Sagadraco mused, "I could see where discovering a source of naturally occurring crystals capable of generating similar or identical power would be extremely desirable."

"And for all its power," Claire said, "the cube can be

destroyed. Not easily, but it can be done. We've had less than a day with the crystal, but we have found no such weakness."

"Nor will you," Tam told her. "From the Heart of Nidaar itself down to specimens the size of the stone in my ring, all are indestructible."

He proceeded to tell Claire and Ben what he knew of the crystal and its motherstone, the Heart of Nidaar.

Claire nodded as she took all of it in. "Unlike the crystal, the cube has power limits. And fortunately, at least for the southern portion of Manhattan, its function can be disrupted."

"How so?" Tam asked.

"Ian's ancestor was a demigod with a magic spear," Rake told him. "Ian has it now. He stabbed the cube just before it was about to explode."

Tam accepted Rake's explanation with a casual nod that said volumes about the level of weirdness he must be exposed to on a daily basis back home.

"May I remove the crystal from the case?" Tam asked Claire.

"Are you sure?"

"I am."

"Very well." Claire keyed in a code, and the lock disengaged with a click. She opened the lid and stepped aside.

Tam stuck his bare-naked hand right in the box and picked up the crystal. No hesitation, even less fear.

The flickering continued just as it had before.

"Unless it is activated and directed to action," he told us, his dark eyes on the stone, "it is harmless."

Ian nodded. "Like C4. You can make bunny rabbits out of it."

That tidbit from my partner's past earned him some odd looks.

He shrugged. "Sometimes you get bored waiting for the action to start."

Somehow I couldn't visualize Ian the commando sitting in the dark, making C4 bunny rabbits, waiting for the signal to blow something up.

"C4?" Tam asked quizzically.

"An explosive," Ian clarified. "A putty consistency."

Tam's lips twitched at the corners. "I know someone who would enjoy learning all about that." He held the crystal out to Ben. "Short-term exposure to such a small stone is perfectly safe. You're a gem mage and this is a natural crystal. There will be no harm."

Ben made no move to take it. "Short-term exposure?"

"The Cha'Nidaar people lived beneath a mountain that was basically lined with these crystals. The motherstone filled an entire cavern. Continuous exposure for years at such a level made them essentially immortal—and sterile."

There was some uneasy muttering at that, and a couple of the guys took a big step back.

"We've determined that casual contact is perfectly safe," Tam added.

Ben didn't look like he was getting any closer any time soon. "What does it do to non-goblins?"

"It is the same. I've seen both elf and human gem mages hold these to no ill effect. Its only response will be a quickening of the flicker and perhaps a warmth coming from it."

A warmth going straight to your nether regions, the guys who took a step back had to be thinking.

"Well, if you're holding it—and wearing another one…" With a "here goes nothing" look, Ben took the stone. Apprehension faded, and a smile grew.

"Now, inject a small portion of your gem magic into the crystal," Tam told him, his voice the only sound in the now silent lab. I think everyone else was holding their breath.

Ben did, and the crystal brightened and glowed like a tiny, well-behaved sun.

Ben ran his thumb slowly across the crystal's surface as if petting it. "This just might be the coolest thing ever." He gave a little gasp. "It's vibrating. Is that normal?"

"Agata got the same reaction," Tam said with a smile. "She compared it to a cat's purr."

I was amazed. "It likes being petted."

Dr. Ben Sadler was grinning like a little boy. "I think it likes me."

"I can't think of any reason why it wouldn't," Tam told him.

"Okay, Ben has a new pet rock," I said. "Now what?"

Tam's smile vanished. "Now we have a few words with our Khrynsani prisoner."

10

Sitting down with a police sketch artist didn't usually come with a side order of anxiety.

You sat down, described the guy you saw, and hoped the sketch came out looking somewhat like the perp and not Homer Simpson.

A session with Susan Connolly would be quick, easy, and uncannily accurate, with none of the frustration that came with having the results look nothing like the guy who stole your purse—or in my case, tried to vaporize me.

Suzy would put her fingertips on my temples, and while I remembered everything I could about who I'd seen, she'd pop into my head and watch my memory movie along with me.

Easy peasy. Pass the popcorn.

At the same time, it was seriously creepy.

Fortunately, Suzy was an absolute doll, sweet as could be, and everyone at SPI loved her. Plus, I'd been told that you couldn't even feel her rummaging around in there, though a couple of agents had said that it tickled.

I could live with that, even if my nerves didn't share my opinion.

Suzy was still at lunch, so her assistant made us comfy in her office.

And yep, I said "us."

Rake and Ian were with me. Tam had gone ahead to Bert's lab to start the preparations for the interrogation. Gethen had given him the Khrynsani's lifestone, because he had somewhere he had to be—namely standing guard outside Suzy's office door.

We'd told Rake what had happened last night and this morning as it related to the mystery goblin who'd tried to turn me into another pile of ashes in what was left of his house. Ever since then, Rake's expression had been set on perma-scowl.

"I don't think Suzy will like you looming over her shoulder while she sketches," I told him. "Not to mention you might not even recognize the guy." I was careful not to say, "*know* the guy."

That was why Ian was here, or at least part of the reason. My partner was all about protecting me—on and off duty. He was starting to come around as far as Rake was concerned, but deep down, when it came to me, he trusted Rake about as far as he could drop-kick him. It wasn't logical or due to anything Rake had done, it was just Ian's protective, big brother instincts, which had nothing to do with logic.

Being a spymaster for goblin intelligence on our world,

Rake knew an inordinate number of shady characters, though describing them as merely "shady" was giving them the serious benefit of a doubt.

Rake seemed convinced that if this goblin had been hanging around his burning house last night, and had tried to vaporize his girlfriend this morning, chances were better than average that he'd be able to put a name to the face I'd be remembering and Suzy would be drawing. And if the goblin revenge gods—yes, they had them—were smiling upon him today, he'd be able to have the guy's head on a platter before sundown.

Ian's problem was that this less than shining example of a law-abiding citizen was still gunning for Rake, and by extension, me. A larger problem was that there were more Khrynsani where this one had come from. Rake was concerned about that, too. Rake's worrying didn't lessen Ian's worrying, and between the two of them, I'd be lucky if I ever got to pee by myself again.

More than once, Rake had mentioned hiring bodyguards for me. I didn't like the idea, but I acknowledged the potential need. I'd given Rake permission with the caveat that I not know they were there.

The grin Rake had given me said "challenge accepted" loud and clear. He'd worked fast. That afternoon, when I'd left SPI HQ, I'd sensed being protectively followed, but danged if I could see anyone. I decided I could live with that, but only when I was off duty. On duty, there were Ian and my equally qualified coworkers.

After this morning, I was rethinking that restriction. I knew Rake was, too.

Suzy rushed in. "My apologies, I usually eat at my desk.

The one day I don't…" She gave a little smile and threw up her hands. "Have you had lunch?" she asked me.

"I've been a little busy this morning."

"So I heard." She pulled up a chair and sat down directly opposite me, our knees nearly touching. "Let's see what we can do to keep that from happening again."

"I'm all for that."

"I asked about lunch because some people get a little nauseated coming out of a link."

Lovely. "I didn't know that."

"It's rare, but it has happened."

"I get dizzy standing up too fast, and I can't fly without being tanked up on Dramamine. And depending on turbulence, I've *still* gotten sick. When I get in a plane, first thing I do is check for an airsick bag."

"Oh dear."

"Yeah. What's the plan for that? Do you keep airsick bags around?"

In response, Suzy reached over and pulled a small plastic-lined trash can over to the left of my chair. She tried a little smile. "How's your aim?"

"Good, from entirely too much practice."

"I couldn't ask for more." She was suddenly all business as she glanced from Ian to Rake and back again. "Gentlemen, this will be much easier for me if you waited outside."

To my amazement, both men stood and left without a word. Impressive.

"Did Mr. Moreau tell you that I only *think* I *might* have gotten a glimpse of the guy?" I asked when Ian had closed the door behind them.

"He did. I may need to tap a deeper level of your sub-conscious; but if you saw him, I'll see him."

"Let me guess, deeper level means increased chance of getting sick."

She reached over for a remote on her desk and dimmed the lights. "It does increase the odds."

"Great, but if we find this guy, it'll be worth it." I closed my eyes and took what I hoped would be a deep, calming breath. "Let's do this."

Suzy placed her fingertips on my temples. I didn't know if she closed her eyes. I wasn't going to check.

"I need you to tell me exactly what happened. What you saw."

I did, concentrating on what I'd seen when I'd alerted Gethen and had looked up to find the goblin watching both of us. Things had happened quickly after that, the goblin's attack and his escape taking no more than a few seconds.

"Are you seeing this?" I murmured.

"I am. Go back a little further to just before you first saw him. You're safe, so don't be afraid to dig deep and relive it. Remember the scents and sounds in addition to what you saw and heard."

Suzy really did have a soothing voice. I wondered if she was also a hypnotist. I let it calm and guide me, as she talked me through what we were both seeing, helping me notice things I hadn't been aware of this morning. Amazingly enough, over all the brimstone and smoke stink, I'd smelled fresh-baked bagels.

My stomach growled. I winced. "Sorry."

Suzy didn't miss a beat; she kept going.

When I again reached the moment of the attack, I tried to slow the action.

Her fingertips tightened slightly. "Don't. Let it happen. I'll do the work."

I did, reaching and passing the point when the goblin activated and stepped through the portal.

"Once more."

I went through the attack and disappearance again. When I reached the instant the goblin touched the cuff on his wrist, I felt what Suzy meant by tapping a deeper level. The image, frozen in time, revealed the goblin's true appearance. I didn't know if the energies from the transporter cuff briefly overpowered his glamour, or if he'd simply gotten cocky and let it drop. It didn't matter. I had him. *We* had him.

He was tall with a swimmer's build, like most goblins. His hair was loose and fell to his shoulder blades. As to his face… Well, let's just say he was easy on the eyes, and could give Rake and Tam a run for their money. I didn't think I'd have any trouble recognizing him if I saw him again.

Suzy brought me back out of whatever trance she'd held me in and did her best to bring me in for a smooth landing. But like a sudden drop during descent into JFK, it wasn't enough to prevent what happened next.

I made sure I leaned to the left.

I was sure Suzy and her cute pink blouse appreciated my aim.

While Suzy sketched, she did not allow Rake to look over her shoulder.

He had asked.

She had refused.

Rake had gotten me a cup of water, and a cold washcloth for my face and neck. Actually, it was a pile of wet and wrung-out paper towels from the nearest bathroom sink, but I wasn't being choosy. If it was cold and wet, it was wonderful.

Ian had gone to the cafeteria for ginger ale and saltines. He hadn't gotten back yet.

Suzy had kept apologizing. "I'm so sorry," she said for the umpteenth time. "Your glimpse of him was so brief, I had to stop you at precisely that time."

And it'd felt like going down the big hill of a giant rollercoaster and when I'd reached the bottom, Suzy had slammed on the brakes.

I rested my forehead in my hand holding the paper towels and tried not to move. "Honey, if you can give us a sketch that helps us catch this guy, it'll be worth it." I raised my head. Slowly. While focusing my eyes on the corner of her desk. "And if you didn't get enough detail and need to go in again, I'm good with that. I'll take vomiting over vaporized any day."

"Oh, I got enough detail. I think you'll be pleased."

That was Rake's cue. "Only if I know the bastard and can get my hands on him within the hour."

Suzy was still sketching when the door opened, and Ian came in with my ginger ale and saltines—the nectar and ambrosia of the gastro-gods.

I all but groaned in relief and gratitude. "Bless your heart. Gimme. Gimme."

"Almost finished?" Ian asked Suzy.

"Almost."

My partner remained standing in front of the door. "Rake, if you know him, we need to do this right."

"Right? The bastard nearly—"

"I know what he nearly did. I was there, remember?"

Rake remembered, and that was part of the reason for his hair-trigger temper right now. He hadn't been there, and as illogical as it was, he blamed himself for what had happened, or what had nearly happened. All Gethen had been able to do was block and redirect the fireball. In his condition this morning, Rake wouldn't have been able to do even that much, and it was eating him up.

"This isn't just about an attempt on Mac's life," Ian continued. "We don't know anything yet, and if you go off half-cocked and obliterate this guy, that's one less source of information. We need him alive."

Rake huffed a dark laugh. "Not if he's wearing a lifestone."

"Alive, Rake."

Suzy's pencil stopped, and she immediately had our attention. Rake's eyes reminded me of a lion on a *Nat Geo* special about to rip the guts out of a gazelle.

Suzy turned the sketchpad around and showed us her work.

Rake hissed. Surprisingly, so did Ian.

I looked and leaned forward to get a closer look. "He looks familiar."

"He should," Ian told me. "Marek Reigory is one of the seven megamages on SPI's most-watched list."

Now I remembered. Ms. Sagadraco had shown them to me last year and told me to memorize their faces. I'd failed that test, but in my defense, one of them had just launched a fireball at me this morning. Marek Reigory had been exiled here from the goblin home world, so it wasn't like he'd be going away any time soon.

Then I remembered something else and felt even sicker than I already was.

Ms. Sagadraco had said a mage from this group was likely responsible for the deaths of SPI's previous three seers—and one of them had just taken a shot at me.

I didn't want to ask what I was about to ask, but I had to know. "Uh, Rake, honey? Don't take this the wrong way, but are you related to Marek Reigory in any way? Even distantly?"

"Absolutely not."

"You're sure?"

"Beyond positive. Why?"

"When I sensed him last night, and ran into him this morning, there was something about him that felt…I don't know how to describe it—"

Rake's expression darkened. "Felt like me?"

Okay, that was unexpected. "Yeah," I said slowly. "Why would he?"

"Blood."

"Excuse me?"

"A couple of years ago, as a result of a confrontation that does not bear going into here, Marek and I fought and tried to kill each other. It was extremely ugly. Magically speaking, we're evenly matched. I think we each wanted the satisfaction of a more physical kill. Knives were used, blood was shed, the fight deteriorated into grappling…"

"Your blood got into Reigory's system," Ian said.

"And his into mine. Mage blood is potent. It didn't take much."

"Blood brothers," Ian surmised.

"So to speak."

None of that answered my question. "I can sense you because you're…we're…well, you know." Even though Ian knew Rake and I were sleeping together, I wasn't about to come right out and say it.

Rake's mouth kicked up a little. "Yes, darling, I *do* know."

"How does that explain how I can sense Mar—" I stopped. "So I can…even though we've never…" Oh boy, did I need to stop. I cringed. "Oh, that's not right."

"I agree."

"And he can sense me?"

"Probably."

"Okay, I need that link to go away. Now."

"Once Marek's dead, it will."

"Not until then?"

"No." Rake's mouth turned into a firm line. "Rest assured, my darling, Marek Reigory's timely demise is my new life's goal."

Once my initial revulsion at my connection with Marek had lessened to prolonged disgust and marginal fear, a new worry reared its head.

"Couldn't Marek use your blood link to try to kill you? Again."

Rake shook his head. "Not without killing himself. It's a self-preservation mechanism. Your own magic won't let you destroy yourself. It also protects me against some of Marek's magic. However, it does the same for him."

Like being magical blood brothers with a mage who'd already tried to kill me twice wasn't bad enough, now Rake was going to question the ghost of a goblin Nazi.

11

If the Khrynsani on Bert Ferguson's examination table hadn't already been dead, Rake would have killed him.

Rake's fangs were fully extended as he paced outside of Bert's workroom. Cancel that. He was stalking. Pacing meant you were nervous. Stalking meant you were nearly homicidal. He had a cut on his bottom lip from his fangs after a particularly emphatic word, but he either didn't notice or didn't care. Marek Reigory had tried to kill me, and he was connected in some way to the dead Khrynsani on Bert's table. Rake couldn't get his hands on Marek, at least not yet, but for the moment he was willing to settle for his accomplice.

I was more or less recovered and had stopped by the ladies' room to floss and brush my teeth within an inch of their life. I hadn't bothered with a Dramamine before Suzy's link because it would have meant waiting at least half an hour for it to take effect. I'd popped one once I knew I was finished being sick. The pill would stay down now and actually do me some good. In the past few minutes, I'd started to feel hungry, which was always an encouraging sign.

I did not want to be here. It wasn't my job; it was more of a package deal.

I was a seer, not a necromancer. But I was Rake's girlfriend, and the dead Khrynsani on Bert's examination table knew why his house had been targeted. If we were lucky, he'd know that, plus why and how Marek Reigory was involved.

Rake had tried to get me to stay out of the observation room, but I'd insisted, and Rake didn't push back. I think on some level, he wanted me here with him.

I'd seen Bert Ferguson raise the dead a few times now, and while I wasn't in a hurry to repeat any of those experiences, at least I'd been in the observation room for all but one of them.

"I'd tell you to be careful, but it sounds like you're doing all you can."

"We are," Rake assured me.

"Do you really think something's gonna go wrong?"

"Nothing will go wrong. We're preparing for the *unexpected*. Khent Mendiu didn't get his job and live as long as he did without being very creative."

In the past, I'd been present when Rake had worked some serious dark magic, but never had he felt the need to wear a robe.

He wore one now. That's what he'd brought from home in his duffel bag.

It was black, it shimmered like silk, and it was thickly

embroidered with what Rake had just told me were protective spells worked with sterling silver thread.

I reached out and straightened the robe's high collar, pulling it closer around his neck. Then I started fiddling with the clasp, checking that the two ends were firmly attached.

Rake's hands covered mine. His were warm and steady. Mine were cold and shaking a little. Rake slowly kissed each of them, one after the other. Then he went back for seconds.

"It will be fine." His voice was soft and reassuring. At least he meant it to be reassuring. I wasn't buying it. "In addition to being chancellor, Tam is also the chief mage and magical enforcer to the royal House of Mal'Salin, a title bestowed on him by our new king's mother, Queen Gilcara, one of the most brilliantly Machiavellian monarchs our people have ever had."

"You say that like it's a good thing."

Rake gave me a quick, wicked grin. "For goblins, it's the highest compliment."

"If you say so."

"The goblin court makes *Game of Thrones* look like a nursery school recess. Tam served as Gilcara's chief mage and enforcer for *five years*."

"I take it that's impressive?"

"The Mal'Salin dynasty goes back over a thousand years. During that time, there have been only four chief mages who were not assassinated. Tam is one of them. The vast majority of chief mages do not live past their first year of service. Tam served for five years before he left."

"So, he's got some dirty tricks up his sleeves."

"He wrote the book." Rake tried a smile for me. "Best

of all, he's my cousin and he likes me. I'll be fine. It'll be over quickly. Khent Mendiu will try to escape, rather than be questioned. Since we'll have to force his soul back into his body and hold it there, it'll be a burnt body trying to escape. You don't have to stay and watch that."

My hands tightened on his. "I'm not going anywhere," I said with more conviction than my feet felt. They wanted to run far and run fast. I winced. "Though I might glance away from time to time if pieces and parts start falling off. Ain't nobody needing to see that. Besides, I just took my last Dramamine. Don't wanna tempt fate too much."

Rake pressed his lips together against a grin. "Understandable. If I wasn't in there with Khent Mendiu, I'd want to look away, too."

I squeezed his hands again. "But you will be, so you can't."

"No, I can't." His eyes were intent on mine. "Makenna, I've done this before, and I will be doing it again."

"You've got a crappy job. You should start looking for another one."

"I think I'll keep this one." He leaned forward and brushed his lips against mine. "It's got great benefits."

Someone cleared his throat behind us.

It was Gethen.

"We're ready when you are, sir."

I gave Rake a quick kiss. "Get it done and get out of there."

Rake had said, and Tam had confirmed, that this was likely to get ugly fast. Khent Mendiu was in the Khrynsani leader's inner circle. You didn't rise to the upper echelons of evil sorcerers by being a magical wuss. This goblin would be powerful even in death. Tam said they were in for a fight, and it'd be a challenge to get any information out of him before his soul started to dissipate.

Bert had raised a dead goblin before, and according to Rake, an evil goblin who had been a Khrynsani was even worse than an evil goblin who'd been a lawyer.

Our staff necromancer was big and tall, and his hair and beard were both white. He was one of those down-to-earth, nice guys that everyone liked to be around—including kids and dogs. And in my opinion, kids and dogs possessed the wisdom of the ages when it came to recognizing bad people on sight. They all loved Bert, which had confirmed for me that Bert wasn't just good people, he was great people.

Naturally, he played Santa Claus for the agents' kids at SPI family holiday parties. Plus, in his day job at SPI, Bert saw dead people, and he could bring them back and talk to them.

Let's see Kris Kringle do that.

Bert would run the show, doing what he called a PML—post-mortem link. I'd seen him do them before. All had been skin-crawling creepy. Once Bert had found himself on the wrong end of a demon-possessed corpse and had nearly died. That would have scared me clear into another career. Not Bert. His next PML a day later had been to get a statement from the aforementioned dead and extremely pissed goblin lawyer. Yeah, Bert had some big ones.

Bert didn't go in for robes, but he was wearing his necroamulet to give him even more protection in addition to his personal shields. Bert was more of a plaid flannel shirt, jeans, and work boots kind of guy, and he wasn't making an exception for an evil goblin mage. Considering that Rake and Tam had opted for robes, I kind of wished Bert had, too, even if it'd been a plaid flannel bathrobe.

Two of Rake's guards who I'd gotten to know over the past few months were stationed just inside the room at the two exits—the door to the observation booth and the door to the main lab.

Rake hadn't brought in his own necromancer. He respected Bert's skill and trusted him to reunite the dead Khrynsani's soul with his body. He and Tam needed to save their strength to hold and question it. Gethen was there for protection for Rake, Tam, and Bert.

All of that said a lot about the Khrynsani mage whose soul they were about to force back into his dead body and interrogate, and none of it was good.

I was in the small observation room behind thick glass that wasn't glass and was supposed to be every kind of proof that our R&D mages could think of: bulletproof, impact proof, fireproof, and most important now, angry goblin ghost proof. SPI's security mages had warded Bert's workroom out the wazoo.

Ms. Sagadraco was here as well, along with Ian. The last burnt goblin Bert had raised hadn't been a particularly nice person in life, but he hadn't been the right hand of the leader of a brotherhood of goblin Nazis and an expert in black magic.

None of us knew what to expect—at least none of us in the observation room. Rake and Tam seemed to know exactly what they were letting themselves in for. I'd never seen Rake so solemn and focused.

Rake and Tam were with Bert at the table. The body

was uncovered. I'd taken one look and decided there was no reason for me to take another.

No one was really concerned that the Khrynsani's soul would escape. The danger was that the soul would escape its own body and force itself into the body of one of the mages in the room. With the exception of Bert, they were all powerful dark mages. Rake had hired Gethen and the two guards because they were the best, and if they were possessed by Khent Mendiu, SPI's entire headquarters complex was in for a heap of trouble.

Bert was also a Vatican-trained exorcist, but even he might be out of his league if the worst happened.

Rake and Tam had agreed that Tam should do any direct contact, since he actually knew Khent Mendiu, and was the best one to identify any images that would flash across the dead goblin's mind.

Tam placed the goblin's lifestone in the center of the corpse's chest. He was standing on the right side of the table, Rake on the left. Bert had taken his usual place at the head, and Gethen stationed himself at the foot. Gethen was close enough to Rake to protect, but far enough away to not be in the way of the work that was about to begin.

"Khent Mendiu."

Bert's deep voice filled the room, commanding the Khrynsani's soul to leave the lifestone.

The stone began to pulse with the same red light that it had glowed with last night, but other than that, nothing happened. It was as if Bert was knocking, and the goblin was home, but there was no way he was opening the door. He knew who was waiting on the other side and he wasn't coming out.

"Khent Mendiu!"

With Bert's second invocation, he filled the goblin's name with the full force of his necromantic power. Even I could feel the pull of it.

The lifestone's glow brightened and the pulse quickened. The goblin was determined to defy the call. I couldn't help but visualize Khent Mendiu behind a door, pushing on it with all his strength to keep it closed.

"Khent Mendiu!"

Bert's voice cracked like a whip and the lifestone shattered on the goblin's chest as a black mist erupted from the stone and Khent Mendiu's soul made a break for it.

Rake and Tam were waiting and ready to pounce. Their hands were already raised and crackling with red energies. The goblin's soul tried to shoot through the lattice of crackles, but Tam and Rake instantly increased the force of their magic, the red glow almost too bright to look at as it solidified into an orb, the goblin's soul trapped inside.

Rake and Tam's hands closed around the trap their collective power had formed, and without any incantation or fancy hocus-pocus, they simply shoved Khent Mendiu's soul, trap and all, into his burnt and blackened body.

I released a breath I hadn't realized I was holding and dropped into one of the room's chairs.

Now it was time for that chat.

The empty eye sockets and nostrils blazed red with the containment spell that now filled the corpse and blocked the exits. The corpse's mouth opened, exposing more red light, as blackened flakes of skin fell to the stainless-steel table.

My stomach held firm. I was proud of it.

What remained of Khent Mendiu's lips peeled back from

fangs that amazingly were still white, in stark contrast to the rest of him.

The corpse thrashed and shouted words in Goblin. Magic had to have been in play here since the corpse no longer had vocal chords. Some I recognized, most I did not. Goblins had a lot of cuss words, and it sounded like Khent Mendiu had a most complete vocabulary.

Tam wasted no time getting down to business.

One thing I hadn't anticipated, though it should have been obvious. If Khent Mendiu knew English, he wasn't speaking it, or in his case shrieking it as he verbally laid into Tam. Tam's rapid-fire questions were in Goblin. My skills in that language were improving, but at the speed Tam was talking, I couldn't catch a single word.

After less than a minute, the shrieking stopped, and the body stilled as it began to fold in on itself.

Rake shouted something to Tam and moved his hands from Khent Mendiu's chest to either side of his head.

Oh no.

I jumped to my feet and immediately regretted it.

Rake linked his mind with what was left of Khent Mendiu's, leaving Tam to keep the fading soul in its body for as long as he could.

Moments later, Rake broke the link, dropping his hands from the goblin's head to grab the table as his legs buckled. Gethen was there to catch him, his arm around Rake's chest as he extended his personal shields to cover his boss.

Tam released the containment field as the body collapsed into a man-sized pile of ash. From the word he hissed, he hadn't gotten what he wanted.

12

Rake recovered more quickly than I would have thought, but more slowly than I hoped.

At least he wasn't possessed.

The dead goblin's soul had vaporized as if it'd been hit by one of Marek Reigory's fireballs.

I wasn't sure if Rake was more bothered that he'd gotten his psychic *tuckus* handed to him by a dead guy, or by what he'd seen while he was in the dead guy's head.

"It's impossible," Rake was saying. "Marek and Isidor Silvanus can't be on the same continent without trying to kill each other, let alone stand next to each other."

That was a name I could've done without hearing again. Isidor and his little brother Phaeon had masterminded what'd happened at the Regor Regency.

"They do like killing up close," Tam admitted. "Though I can say the same for myself, except I merely want to make sure what I kill stays that way."

"When Khent saw them, they weren't killing each other or anyone else," Rake said. "They were talking to Sandrina Ghalfari, which is worse."

"That's a trio that should not be together."

"That's what I saw," Rake insisted. "Sandrina gave Isidor a whole trunk full of crystals, and he gave her two chests like the one Tulis saw in my house."

"I'm not disputing what you saw, I'm agreeing that it's bad. Khent's soul was fading, but you had a good, solid link with him. Any memory you accessed would've been accurate."

"Did you get any indication of where they were?" Ms. Sagadraco asked Rake.

"No, but it would have had to have been on this world. Marek can't leave."

"House arrest ankle bracelet?" I asked. "Or in his case, a world arrest ankle bracelet?"

"It's more like the goblin version of a tracking microchip, except this one would instantly kill him if he tried to leave the planet."

"But when I saw him this morning, he teleported right out of there."

"It would have been to somewhere on Earth."

"He's exiled from your world, yet your people gave him free rein on ours." Ian was leaning against the doorway, his arms crossed and mood dark.

I snorted. "Yeah, I don't think any of us are feeling the love right now."

"I'm in complete agreement," Rake said. "Marek should have been executed long ago. His family used their influence to get his sentence reduced to exile." He flashed a grin. "The good news is, now that I'm the governor of the goblin colony here, changing Marek's sentence is well within my authority. My predecessor looked the other way while Marek broke any law he desired. His attack on Makenna was attempted murder, and his meeting with Sandrina was collusion with a convicted and condemned traitor to the goblin crown. Marek's life is legally mine as soon as I can take it. Sandrina already has a death sentence on her head. Isidor has committed many crimes, but has yet to be tried and convicted, though I don't plan to let that little detail get in my way once I get my hands on him."

"What you saw sounds like an arms deal," Ian noted. "A nuclear-level arms deal. The previous version of the magetech generator filled the trunk of a car. It looks like Phaeon has managed to make it smaller."

"Magetech generator 2.0," I muttered. "Just what we didn't need."

"What is this magetech generator?" Tam asked.

Rake gave his cousin the condensed version of what had happened at the Regor Regency.

Scooping an entire hotel—and all the staff, diplomat guests, and SPI agents inside—out of Lower Manhattan and into a pocket dimension hadn't been magical small potatoes. It had been a serious magical working—with a heaping helping of the latest technology. We'd known that Isidor Silvanus had a knack for conjuring pocket dimensions, but to whisk a building that covered nearly an entire city block out of our world and into a pocket of alternate reality would be impossible for any mage—or so we'd thought. We didn't even suspect Isidor, until Kenji and I had seen Isidor's tech genius brother Phaeon and his latest gadget. Only then did we realize who was behind the conjuring and whisking. We'd only survived thanks to the combined magical talent, technical knowledge, and death-defying determination of those of us imprisoned inside.

No doubt the Silvanus brothers had been very disappointed.

And for the ultimate middle finger, not only had we stopped the magetech generator from killing us all, we'd disabled it and taken it home with us to study. That had probably turned their disappointment to frothing-at-the-mouth rage.

At least that was my assumption. We hadn't seen hide nor hair of the Silvanus brothers since then. We'd been sure we'd be hearing from them soon. They were way too pissed off at us to stay under the radar for long.

This was one time I really hadn't wanted us to be right.

"If what's moving buildings isn't a smaller version of a magetech generator, that means Phaeon came up with something new," Ian was saying. "I hope he merely shrank it. With his previous version in our lab, our people can figure out how it works—and how to make it *not* work—regardless of size."

"I need to alert Imala to the possibilities," Tam said. "Sandrina could have used Rake's house as a test. The Khrynsani's next target could be the royal palace or the citadel on the Isle of Mid. Either would be a catastrophic loss."

"Sandrina gave Isidor what amounts to a bushel basket of those crystals," I reminded them. "If Isidor gave her two generators, who knows how many Phaeon has made and they have stashed away here? Six buildings have vanished already—that we know of. And they're in places where they either wouldn't be missed, or it'd take awhile for anyone to notice. If those aren't tests for something big, I don't know what is. It sounds like the Khrynsani are up to no good back home, but what are the Silvanus brothers planning for *our* world?"

Silence met that happy thought.

"I understand Isidor making nice with this Sandrina Ghalfari," Ian said, "but how does Marek Reigory fit in?"

"Marek's ambition is what got him exiled," Rake told him. "His misbehavior has continued here unabated." He glanced at Ms. Sagadraco, as if asking permission to continue. Ian and his scowl silently followed the exchange. I knew in his mind this would go down as just one more thing Rake had kept from us.

Our boss exhaled slowly. "I will take it from here, Lord Danescu. We have had reports of the mages on our most-watched list being seen together, mostly in pairs and mainly in Europe. Eight months ago, five of them were in Prague the same week. They were never seen together, but that didn't mean a meeting didn't take place. Three months ago, the same five mages, with the notable addition of Marek Reigory, were in Amsterdam."

"And a month later, the Silvanus brothers took the Regor Regency hostage," Ian said. "Coincidence?"

"We're not treating it as one, Agent Byrne. I have reason to believe these mages have formed a cabal of sorts. For what purpose, we do not yet know, but I believe the events of the past day have given us a glimpse into the reason behind those clandestine meetings."

"Their clandestine is my clueless," I said. "Aside from the fact that at least one of them wants me dead. When the Khrynsani dropped Rake's house on us last night, I got the feeling Marek wasn't amused. That doesn't sound like the flawless execution of an evil master plan."

Rake almost smiled. "You understand more than you know, darling Makenna. Your two encounters with Marek have given us invaluable insight."

"I'm still in the fog."

Rake leaned forward. "You said that Marek seemed angry last night, and anxious bordering on desperate this morning while searching for the crystal."

"Yes."

"I think the fire that destroyed my house was an accident, and possibly the taking of the house itself. Marek is the only goblin member of the cabal that we're aware of. Would you say that is still correct, Madame Sagadraco?"

"My sources have reported no other goblin."

"Are you sure he isn't acting independently?" Ian asked.

"All but positive," Rake said.

"How do you know?"

"He tried to recruit me as the second goblin in their little club."

I blinked. "What?"

"It was years ago, dearest. Before I met you." He gave Ms. Sagadraco an amused glance. "Vivienne was quite put out that I refused his offer."

"Excuse me?"

"It is always useful to have someone on the inside, Agent Fraser," Ms. Sagadraco explained.

"Useful, but time-consuming," Rake said. "I had my hands more than full working for goblin intelligence. I'm answerable to enough people back home."

Tam chuckled. "Imala doesn't share well with others."

"And I don't play well with others. Marek would be the cabal's natural choice to arrange a meeting and deal between Isidor and Sandrina. Marek's family has close ties with the Khrynsani, and Sandrina is their acting leader—"

"I thought you said the Khrynsani are an all-boys club," I said.

"They are. But for Sandrina, they made an exception."

"Is she powerful? Influential? Loaded?"

"All of the above, but mainly she was too evil to pass up. Sandrina and Isidor did not meet and come to *any* kind of agreement on their own. Marek knows both of them. That he was present when the trade took place indicates to me that he was acting as a representative of the cabal."

"Your house burnt, and now the crystal is sitting in our lab rather than the cabal's lair," I surmised. "His cohorts in the evil mage clubhouse probably aren't too happy with him right now."

Rake's eyes sparkled. "No, they're not, and it couldn't have happened to a more deserving guy. I have a feeling the Khrynsani weren't authorized to do what they did. The other building disappearances were in remote locations far from here. Dropping my house onto my lot in the middle of New York is as public as it gets. It sounds like a Khrynsani operation—all of the twisted fun and no blowback on them.

However, my house appearing here with the crystal and possible magetech generator inside just put those six building disappearances squarely on SPI's radar. No, the cabal is not at all happy with the Khrynsani. If Tulis hadn't killed Khent Mendiu, I highly suspect Marek would have gladly done the job."

13

Rake had taken Tam back to his apartment. He was going to talk to his sources/agents to locate Marek, and Tam was going to use the equipment in Rake's lab to report to Imala Kalis and again try to reach Agata Azul.

Ms. Sagadraco had directed Dr. Cheban to focus on the remains of the metal chest found in Rake's house and the metal used in the construction of the magetech generator to determine if there were any similarities.

Ian and I were going to see what Kenji had dug up about the previous building disappearances.

I'd made the mistake of checking Twitter. According to every news source, I was now dating a billionaire, playboy, philanthropist, and superhero.

So much for running under the radar.

When Ian and I got off the elevator on the floor where the agent cube farm was located, I was greeted accordingly.

"Yo, Pepper Potts!" came a shout from somewhere in the middle of the walled warren of offices.

"Bite me!" I yelled back.

That earned me some cheers and whistles.

As we made our way to the far corner and the IT department, Alain Moreau's cultured voice came over the PA: *"A reminder that tomorrow at noon in the cafeteria will be a Lunch and Learn on troll interpersonal relations and cultural taboos. After last week's incident, it's apparent that some of you could use a refresher. It's open to anyone who wants to attend, but for Agent Team Delta, it's mandatory."*

"Ooooh," went up from the bullpen.

The IT center of the SPI universe was in the bullpen's northeast corner—Kenji Hayashi's command center. At least that's what everyone else called it. Kenji just called it his desk.

Kenji's desk was a semicircle lined with a total of twelve huge flat-screen monitors, six on the bottom and six mounted directly above. Behind him within easy reach were shelves stacked with his haul from the latest Comic-Con, binders of compiled research, and gadgets in various stages of completion that he'd whipped up to make the work of our monster-hunting commandos safer. A lot of them were supernaturals, but even they could use technological advantages over the creatures they hunted. During every mission of the New York office's two commando teams, the AV feeds from their helmets came directly to Kenji's screens. He saw what each agent saw and tracked their locations. If someone got into trouble, Kenji could direct the closest team members to help. Our commandos thought of Kenji as their guardian angel.

That angel was presently leaning back in his desk chair, popping wasabi-covered peas from the Mr. Spock candy jar on his desk. The peas were Kenji's idea of getting enough vegetables.

There was another reason we were blessed to have Kenji on our side.

He wasn't a mage, but he was seven different kinds of genius.

There were those who were naturally drawn to tech, and those who had it thrust upon them, usually by a family member, in the form of "you're never gonna get a decent-paying job if you don't know about computers."

Of all those folks, there was a small minority that combined skills and smarts with an above-average level of psychosis. That combination either went on to become a CEO in Silicon Valley, or a villain petting their white cat in a volcanic island lair. Give a person like that access to magic as well, and you had the makings of an interdimensional supervillain, which is what we were dealing with now.

Fortunately for the future of planet Earth and the greater cosmos, Kenji Hayashi was a genius who was also a great guy and allergic to cats.

Phaeon Silvanus, on the other hand, was the founder and CEO of the Hart Group, which included Hart Pharmaceuticals, which, thanks to SPI, was presently under investigation by federal, state, and local authorities. Another company under the Hart Group umbrella was Hart Defense Systems, which had found itself a niche developing smaller, more specialized weapons; an arms boutique, if you will. Hart Defense was presently a darling of the Pentagon, but they also had under-the-table dealings with shadowy foreign interests. Unfortunately, SPI didn't have prosecutable proof that we could pass on to our contacts at the mortal alphabet agencies.

Phaeon's brother, Isidor, was the magic-slinging half of their dastardly dynamic duo.

Now it appeared they'd joined forces with another world's version of Nazis, and our world's version of a real-life SPECTRE or Hydra populated by megamages.

My naturally paranoid imagination skipped further down that dark path to the fact that once Phaeon's magetech generator had been activated, you didn't have to be either a megamage or a tech genius to use it.

That left the psychos with the money and influence to buy one for their very own.

Unfortunately, Earth had no shortage of rich, psychotic megalomaniacs.

And Rake had once told me that the one thing Isidor Silvanus loved more than power was money.

Like we needed more problems.

Kenji loved problems when he could consider them riddles to be solved.

Buildings disappearing using crystals from another world as a power source? Kenji was positively giddy.

On the monitor immediately in front of him was a map of the US with a scattering of red dots. Red was Kenji's go-to color for indicating locations of the weirdness du jour.

Ian and I pulled up chairs.

"That's entirely too many red dots," Ian told him.

"I'm just glad it's not 3D and spinning," I said. My stomach was similarly grateful.

Kenji grinned. "I tried."

"I'm sure you did."

"What about the rest of the world?" Ian asked.

The elf clicked a few keys, and the screen's scope expanded to a worldwide view.

No red dots.

"Still nada," he said. "The US of A has this one all to itself."

"Lucky us," I muttered.

As Kenji closed the window to show only the US, five more dots appeared on the western part of the map, this time in bright green, the runner-up in his cavalcade of colors to indicate evil supernatural activity.

Kenji zoomed in. "Hmm, more greenies coming in. I'm using green to show where similar incidents occurred more than six months ago."

I wasn't sure I'd heard correctly. "Six *months*?"

"You heard it here first. Months."

With the exception of Rake's house here, the rest of the dots were in the southwestern US: Nevada, Utah, Colorado, New Mexico, and Arizona.

Ian leaned forward and did a quick count. "Fourteen in red and seven green. Twenty-one buildings that have vanished as if they never existed, and we're just now hearing about it?"

Kenji shrugged. "The majority happened out in the middle of nowhere or in deserted towns. The disappearances either went unnoticed, or news took time to reach any of our agents."

We told him about the cabal, the Khrynsani, and Marek Reigory.

SPI loved stupid bad guys who all but did our jobs for us. Villains became dead or incarcerated villains by being stupid and doing dumb things. Villains who ran around yelling, "Hey ya'll, watch this!" with every flashy, villainy thing they did, tended to attract attention they didn't want if they wanted to go on being productive villains.

Unfortunately, that wasn't what we had here. The Khrynsani hadn't been stupid. It was more of a "not our world, not our problem" scenario. The house had to go somewhere, why not Rake's vacant lot, the man responsible for booting their colonial governor puppet out of his cushy office?

That brought up a thought.

"Uh, guys? Rake thinks the Khrynsani did what they did pretty much to be a pain in the ass. If the cabal is using these abandoned buildings as tests, they would have to have sent them *somewhere*. The Southwest has a lot of empty spaces. Do you think a tiny piece of that might have twenty-one new buildings?"

"Do we have photos of them?" Ian asked.

"Some." Kenji was nodding and clicking. "As to any new towns springing up with mismatched buildings, let me borrow a couple of satellites and see what I can find."

My partner frowned. "Military satellites?"

"They've got the best ones."

"That's illegal."

"No, it's not. Their own people will be making the path changes. Of course, they won't know about it." Kenji waggled his eyebrows. "Just call me The Glitch."

"I didn't hear this."

The elf flashed a grin. "You couldn't have. I never said it."

"Do any ley lines correlate to the building sites?" Ian asked, taking a sharp right from a former US Special Forces officer witnessing the piracy of US military satellites.

I'd forgotten about that. "That's right. Phaeon's magetech generator needed ley lines to work."

"It's the first thing I checked," Kenji replied. He hit one key and leaned back. "Look at that."

I whistled. "Yowza. It looks like the Rockefeller Center Christmas tree lights all wadded up into a ball."

"Ley lines, energy vortexes, spirit portals, you name it, they're out there. The building sites are divided among them. Since most of the events happened too long ago to have any magic residue left, I'm checking on power outages in the nearest town to determine the likely dates when the buildings vanished."

"Good idea," I told him. "Where do you stand on that?"

"Info is still coming in. Like you said, there's a lot of empty out there. Some of the closest towns have populations of less than fifty. But even in the smallest places, outages get reported, either to the local police or electric cooperative. Don't worry, we'll get what we need."

Kenji's desk phone rang. He glanced at the readout to decide whether to let it roll over to voice mail. Kenji was notorious for not answering his phone unless it was the boss, Mr. Moreau, or worth his time.

He snatched up the receiver. "Hey, Claire." He glanced over at us with a wink. "Yeah, they're right here." He listened for a few moments. "Uh-huh. Well, that makes things interesting. I'll tell them."

"Tell us what?" Ian asked before Kenji had hung up.

"The metallurgy analysis came back. The slag from Rake's house is a ninety-five percent match for the magetech generator's case. Sounds like Phaeon did a fancy upgrade for your goblin Nazis."

14

Two hours later, we got our first big break.

An agent in our Los Angeles office reported a building disappearance that had happened last night. A friend of hers was a location scout for a small film company. She and one of her staff had visited Shiloh City, Nevada, yesterday and had liked what they'd seen. Shiloh City was different than most of the mining boomtowns that'd sprung up throughout the Southwest in the mid- to late 1800s. Its buildings hadn't just been slapped together overnight; as a result, they were substantial enough to withstand a film shoot. At least the exteriors were. They wouldn't be using the interiors; those would be shot on a studio soundstage. But the exteriors were more than stable enough not to fall on cast or crew during shooting.

They'd rented an RV and had camped nearby. Last night,

all of their electronic devices had lost power for over an hour, and they'd been treated to a light show in the sky. They'd chalked it up to some kind of solar flare thing. Once the glow in the sky faded, their power came back on, and they went back to sleep. When they'd woken up this morning, the hotel that'd been there yesterday was gone. Not gone as in collapsed into a pile of rubble. Gone as in it had never existed.

The location scout immediately took pictures of the now-vacant lot and called her SPI agent buddy.

Within twenty-four hours was the ideal timeframe to find strong remnants of whatever mutant lovechild of magic and technology had been used there.

Our LA agent forwarded the photos her friend had taken of the hotel and surrounding town. I didn't know what kind of movie they'd planned to shoot there, and for our purposes, it really didn't matter.

Gone was gone.

Kenji had forwarded the photos to me and Ian. As I flipped through them on my phone, there wasn't a brick or board left to say the town's hotel had ever been there.

Normal folks would probably say "spooky," but when you work for an organization like SPI, "spooky" takes on a whole new meaning. Things would have to get a lot weirder to qualify.

Whoever had built the Shiloh City Hotel had put a lot of work into it. It was a two-story, red brick Victorian. Amazingly, the hotel's tall windows had been intact, with no glass missing that I could see. Through the ornate double doors had been a lobby with a curved staircase against one wall that presumably led up to the guest rooms on the second floor.

On either side of it had been a saloon and restaurant. The

three buildings had been constructed separately, but according to the location scout, a Boston entrepreneur had bought all three in 1888 and had connected them by knocking out the walls in between. By converting the holes in the walls into arched doorways, he'd made the Shiloh City Hotel a Wild West precursor to Las Vegas, a couple hundred miles to the south. Eat, drink, sleep, and gamble all in one place.

Only now it was a place that didn't exist anymore—at least not in Shiloh City.

Ian frowned as he scrolled through the photos Kenji had sent us of the other buildings that had disappeared. He had gotten word back about power outages close to six of the disappearances. The Shiloh City Hotel made seven. Information on seven out of twenty-one wasn't great, but it at least gave us something to work with.

The hotel was the largest building so far. The sawmill taken in Colorado had been smaller, but not by much.

It had been gone for five days.

The next building had been taken twelve days ago. It had been marginally smaller than the sawmill.

Ian's eyes scrolled down the list of probable dates and building sizes. "Phaeon's escalating. Each time a larger building."

"But still with no one inside."

"That we know of."

Tam hadn't been able to reach Agata Azul. Since we now had a trail that might actually be followable, we needed to track it while the scent was fresh.

With Ben Sadler.

Tam was confident that our consulting gem mage would be able to help.

Ben was confident that he was having an anxiety attack.

I really couldn't say that I blamed him. If I were in his shoes, I'd probably be hyperventilating, too.

"Honey, you're not gonna be taking on Phaeon, Isidor, a megamage, or a goblin Nazi," I assured him. "You're merely going to use one rock to find another rock. We have people to do all that other stuff." I waved the hand and arm that wasn't presently around his shoulder. "It's what they train for, and quite frankly, they live for it. They're crazy like that."

Tam was tugging his crystal ring off his finger, and I resisted the urge to clamp down on Ben's shoulder to keep him from running away. He wasn't really going to run (at least I didn't think so), and he needed to know that we had the confidence in him that he didn't.

Tam held the ring out to Ben. "Just try it. If it doesn't work, you're off the hook, I believe the phrase goes."

"Okaaay." Ben took the ring and slid it on his finger. As soon as it touched his skin, the flames inside began flickering in what I could only describe as extreme enthusiasm.

"It's a little large," Tam noted, "but we can fix that."

Ben froze and emitted a squeak. "That won't be necessary," he barely whispered, staring down at the entirely too happy rock. "It…constricted."

Yikes.

Tam was calm, at least outwardly. "I should have expected this."

Ben's voice was strangled. "Yes, you should have."

"Can you take it off?"

Ben tried, and to his relief and ours, the ring easily slid off his finger. The crystal's glow dimmed.

"I think you hurt its feelings," I told him.

"That's odd," Tam said.

Ben swallowed with an audible gulp. "I was going to go with 'terrifying,' but that'll work, too."

"It could be an acknowledgment of your gift," Rake ventured.

"Did it do this with Agata?" Ben asked.

"Agata has a pendant; she never tried on the ring."

"Maybe you should consider it a hug," I suggested. I left "from a finger-sized python" unsaid.

Ben wasn't convinced, but he did slide the ring back on his finger. As he took one breath after another, forcing himself to relax, the flames inside the crystal again flickered happily.

"Come to think of it, I have heard of rings of power sizing themselves to those they have accepted," Tam noted.

Ben tried to smile, but it looked more like a grimace. "Just call me Frodo."

"I beg your pardon?" Tam asked.

"Earth literature reference," I said.

"Oh."

"Things didn't go so great for Frodo, but I'm sure this situation will be entirely different."

"Agata didn't experience any adverse reaction to prolonged contact with her pendant," Tam said. "If it weren't for that bond giving her direct contact with the Heart of Nidaar, hundreds of people, myself included, wouldn't be alive right now. We owe that bond our lives."

Ben began to look less unsure of his role in all this. "If you think it will help."

"It may be the only chance we have to find those crystals."

"How close will he have to be for the ring to work?" I asked.

"Agata's pendant began detecting the Heart of Nidaar…" Tam turned to Rake. "How many of your miles are the Laskani Islands from the north coast of Aquas?"

Rake thought for a few moments. "About twelve hundred."

Tam did some mental math of his own. "Then add another two hundred from the coast to the mountain containing the Heart. However, the Heart of Nidaar is enormous."

"So size matters," I said with a straight face.

Rake didn't take the bait. "The area where the events have occurred covers approximately a thousand miles. It can be done. And if we can get even a decent residual from the Shiloh City site, we can start zeroing in on the cabal's home base before they decide they've done enough tests and move on to their real objective."

Alain Moreau had been running a think tank with SPI's brainiacs to try to determine what the cabal could be after. Working from the hypothesis that their home base was somewhere in the five states where the disappearances had taken place, they had determined strategic locations that could be the mages' potential target.

Entirely too many of those possible targets were military.

Cheyenne Mountain, Los Alamos, White Sands, Dugway, Nellis, and who could forget Area 51. Those were just the bigger names. There were dozens of bases, chemical depots, and weapon test sites. Plus, there were the top-secret locations that only select people in the government knew about.

It was a terrorist smorgasbord. And those terrorists were at the top of the evil mage food chain and had allied themselves with beings who were essentially aliens possessing an indestructible and limitless power source.

Yeah, we had to take any clues we had and run with them. Fast.

The size of their target was increasing, and the time between the taking of those targets was decreasing—and so was the time we had left to find their ultimate target and stop them.

"I want you to try something," Tam was saying to Ben. "Using the crystal in the ring, try to sense the two crystals down in the lab."

Ben closed his eyes and took a deep breath. After a few seconds, the flicker of the crystal in the ring slowed in time to a heartbeat, presumably Ben's.

The rest of us were trying not to breathe, at least I was.

Less than a minute later, a slow smile crept over Ben's lips as he opened his eyes. "Oh yeah."

"You got it? Them?" I tried not to sound surprised.

"Loud and *really* clear." He looked at Tam, and his smile widened into a boyish grin. "I can do this."

Tam clapped our gem mage on the shoulder. "I never doubted it."

15

Instead of an SPI jet, we'd take Rake's jet to Nevada. In the human world, one of SPI's jets would be just another corporate plane. In the supernatural world, it would attract attention we didn't want. For that matter, so would Rake's. This particular jet wasn't registered to Rake, at least not directly. Its ownership was buried under half a dozen holding companies. In addition, it was plain as far as corporate jets went, really plain. It all too obviously wasn't the latest and greatest in aviation technology. But there had to be more to it than met the eye. I couldn't imagine Rake owning an avionic piece of crap.

Ben shared my opinion, but took it one step further. He looked downright concerned at our impending mode of transportation. He didn't say anything, but I could tell he doubted the thing was even airworthy.

Rake noticed. "She's got it where it counts, kid."

I snorted a laugh. Hot as hell *with* geek bona fides. I mean, really, how much more could a girl ask for? "I love you."

Rake's eyes gleamed. "I know."

We were at SPI's airfield in Westchester County, north of Manhattan. Now that he was in Vivienne Sagadraco's good graces, she'd allowed Rake to use it as well.

"When I travel," Rake continued, "there are times I don't want to attract attention."

"Mission accomplished," Ian drawled.

We soon discovered the outside of the jet was a disguise for what was inside—in the cabin and under the hood, or whatever it was called on a plane. We not only flew to Nevada in style, we got there fast.

We landed out in the middle of the Nevada desert. At least that's what it looked like. However, once we were on the ground, I saw that the tarmac had been artfully dusted with desert sand. The airstrip had been recently paved, which was at odds with the rusted-out domed building that passed for a hangar.

I glanced from the rusted building to the fresh tarmac beneath my feet and back again. I didn't say a word. I merely gave Rake a sideways glance and raised an eyebrow.

"I am not the only one to appreciate discretion while traveling," he said mysteriously.

"So it only looks like we're out in the middle of nowhere. We're obviously close to somewhere…interesting."

It was Ian who answered. "That would depend on who you ask."

Rake and Ian traded a meaningful look, leaving yours truly

clueless. It wouldn't be the first time they had information that I didn't. Rake was a goblin spymaster. Ian was former Special Forces. Since our landing site wouldn't be the oddest thing we'd encountered today, I kept my curiosity to myself. This was probably one of those "I could tell you, but I'd have to kill you" places.

The mystery continued as Rake gave me a sly grin and, taking my hand, led me to the hangar. "I've arranged a surprise for you."

Next to the side door, Rake pushed back a flap of tin concealing a keypad that wouldn't have looked out of place at SPI. He keyed in a series of numbers, and a much-heavier-than-it-looked door clicked open.

The lights came on automatically, revealing a hangar so shiny and new you could've eaten off the floor. It was empty except for an old military Hummer and a two-door, soft-top Jeep Wrangler.

I squealed. I couldn't help myself.

When I'd moved to New York, I'd had to leave my Jeep back home in the North Carolina mountains.

God, I missed that Jeep.

Rake swept me a little bow. "Your noble steed awaits, my lady."

It took everything I had not to run over and throw myself across the hood in a full-chassis hug. "This is even the model year I have back home."

Rake grinned. "I know."

"I want you now." And I didn't care who heard.

"I know that, too. Hold that thought, we've got work to do first."

The Jeep left a rooster tail of dust as we sped across the late afternoon Nevada desert.

This wasn't exactly what Rake and I had had in mind for our first trip away together, but that didn't stop it from being freakin' awesome.

I was driving, Rake was riding literal shotgun, and Gethen was in what passed for a backseat holding on to the roll bar. He'd said he wasn't letting Rake out of his sight, and to do that he'd insisted on being in the Jeep with us. I was the smallest and would've been a better fit for the backseat, but there was no way in hell I wasn't driving.

Ian, Tam, and Ben were in the Hummer behind us. At least they had been behind us. It hadn't taken long for Ian to get tired of eating our dust. Now he was more or less beside us.

Dr. Cheban had sent a device with Ben that was like a souped-up metal detector. She'd programmed it to home in on even the smallest concentrations of metals found in the magetech generator. Between it and Ben's gem skills, we were hoping to strike it rich in our abandoned mining town.

I felt Rake's eyes on me and risked a quick glance as the Jeep bounced its way over another dip in what passed for a road out here.

"What?" I yelled over to him.

He smiled and shook his head. "Nothing. Just that you haven't stopped grinning since you got behind the wheel."

"I'm not grinning." Then I realized my face hurt from doing just that. Heck, I probably even had bugs between my teeth, because of course, I'd insisted on taking the top off.

It was loud, dusty, and wonderful.

Mud or dust on the driver and Jeep meant you were doing it right. A dust-covered or mud-spattered Jeep was a happy Jeep. Come to think of it, seeing either one of those brought a smile to my face, too.

I grinned even more broadly. "Yep, I've got it bad."

Rake turned to face forward, studying the landscape through our now less-than-clean windshield. He glanced down at the GPS app. Any signal my phone might have scrounged had vanished thirty miles back. Rake and Ian's phones had some kind of turbo-charged satellite link or something.

The wind was starting to pick up, giving me second thoughts about taking the Jeep's top off.

According to what passed for a map of the area, Shiloh City was all that was in the middle of a whole lot of nothing. Based on the information we had, the not-so-distant ridge had been the site of a silver mine back in the mid-1870s. It'd been a big strike, enough to justify the small town that'd sprung up nearby. Calling it a city would be pushing it, but the miners in Shiloh City apparently had civic pride to spare and had named their town accordingly. Once the silver had played out, so had the only reason for the people to stay. They'd gradually gone, leaving the buildings behind.

Ian and I slowed our respective vehicles as the ghost town came into view. We drove slowly down the one street, and stopped in front of the big, empty space in the middle of town. There were buildings on either side, but where the hotel/saloon/restaurant had once stood was bare ground.

I could feel Rake scanning the area to make sure we didn't have company.

"Clear?" I asked.

"Within fifty miles."

"Sense any malicious mumbo-jumbo?"

Rake continued his stare off into the middle distance. He slowly shook his head.

"Any recent portal action?" he asked me.

"Nada."

We got out of the Jeep. Ian and Tam met us in front of where the hotel had been. Ben made his way over, still a little wobbly after our dash across the desert, ring on one hand, Dr. Cheban's metal detector clutched in the other. We all waited for Ben to get his bearings.

As if listening to something only he could hear, Ben walked right through where the hotel's front door had been and proceeded to a spot that, according to the photos, had been about where the front desk had stood. He stopped and looked down.

We all stayed put, not wanting to interfere in any signals the gem mage might be getting.

"It was here," Ben called back to us.

Tam crossed the empty lot to where Ben stood, and the rest of us followed.

Ben was booting up Dr. Cheban's detector. "There's no crystal now, but I can sense that it was here recently."

"Do you have any sense of a direction?" Tam asked.

Ben thought for a few moments, his brow wrinkling with effort. "I know this sounds strange, but it's like the air is too thick."

"It doesn't sound strange at all," Tam told him. "Agata would get her best read once the sun had gone down and the air cooled."

"So, what do we do now?" I asked.

Rake clapped his hands together. "We make camp and have dinner. Who's hungry?"

Tam grinned. "And for our after-dinner entertainment, I'll teach Dr. Sadler how to defeat multiple opponents with a single rock."

16

Rake's idea of roughing it was way different from what I was used to. Tam's idea of self-defense with rocks was a twisted take on Yoda and Luke Skywalker.

The first "tent" Rake put up was a cloaking spell that covered our entire campsite, including our vehicles, and made us invisible and inaudible to anyone in or even above the area. We even had a nice fire going, but if you were standing outside the barrier, all you'd see was a whole lot of dark desert. And a repelling spell thrown in would signal any desert critters to go around and keep right on going. That went for snakes and the two-legged variety as well. In addition, Rake and Tam would know if anyone came within a thousand yards of our little oasis.

We'd come prepared to stay at least one night, and Rake had told us he'd take care of provisions.

As a result, our campsite and meal had five-star ratings.

The tents looked like something out of an REI photo shoot, and the food tasted like it'd come from Rake's hotel restaurant—which it probably had.

We were full and happy, and ready to watch Tam teach Ben the way of the rock, though Ben wasn't particularly thrilled about being watched.

Tam was setting up the targets while Ben casually tossed a roundish rock in a baseball glove. Ian had brought one of his gloves for Ben to use when Tam had told him what he had in mind.

"Agata Azul has a baseball glove?" Ben called to Tam. "Or whatever the equivalent is on your world."

Tam was putting the finishing touches on his targets. He'd found some old bottles and cans lying around and had lined them up on two large rocks that were a good fifty yards from where Ben stood. Rake had extended the campsite's shielding spell to cover Tam's after-dinner fun and games.

"Agata doesn't use a glove, because she can control the speed of a rock when she calls it back to her."

Ben stopped tossing. "Calls it?"

"That's what I said. Until you have that level of control—though I believe it will come quickly—it's safer to protect your hand."

Tam's targets reminded me of my childhood shooting range. It was where a cow pasture ended and thick woods began. My cousins and I had used an old washing machine with cans lined up on top. Select aunts and uncles had been our instructors. That washing machine had ended up with more holes than the cans. Now I spend a lot of quality time at SPI's shooting range to get better with both of my weapons.

I used my paint pistol and rifle more than my real gun and had saved lives with them.

I could see through glamours and veils. Our commando teams could not. Put one rampaging monster that had been rendered invisible by a cloaking spell in a room with our commandos, and you had a recipe for disaster—not to mention death and dismemberment. If I could tag the beastie with glow-in-the-dark paint pellets, our commandos could take it down before it could take them out.

As a result, I took my target practice very seriously.

Ben Sadler didn't have a gun. He had a pile of baseball-sized rocks on the ground next to him. There wasn't anything special about the rocks. Tam had selected them based on what would be a comfortable size for Ben's hands.

"Uh, Chancellor Nathrach—"

"Tam," the goblin called back.

"Tam, I can't throw that far."

"That's the point." Tam finished and walked back to where Ben waited. "You don't have to. You throw the rock *toward* the target to get it going. You tell the rock to go the rest of the way."

"*Tell* the rock?"

"Yes, tell it. Just because you've never done a thing before doesn't mean you can't do it and do it very well. I know a young elf by the name of Piaras Rivalin. He's only a few years younger than you and is one of the three most powerful spellsingers on our world."

"Spellsinger?"

"It's exactly what sounds like. With the power of their voices, spellsingers can influence thought with a hummed phrase, either sung or spoken, or control actions with simple speech or a tune. The number of people is irrelevant. I've seen a spellsinger turn the tide of a battle. They can project to make their voices heard, and anyone within hearing distance will be affected. Piaras once put an entire citadel of knights to sleep with a lullaby."

Ben was quiet for a few moments. "And you think I have that level of talent?"

"I don't think it, I believe and know it. Once you believe it yourself, a whole world of ability will open up to you. You have more talent than you know."

Ben glanced down at the pile of rocks and out at the target, which was a goodly distance away. No problem for a bullet, but for a guy who didn't have a major-league pitching arm? It'd be a bit much.

Tam didn't see any of it as a problem.

"Whenever you're ready, throw the rock in your hand at the target," he told Ben. "Don't think about it, just throw."

"But I—"

"Just humor me."

Ben did.

And the rock landed only halfway to the first target. Heck, I was impressed that it'd gone more or less straight. It was way more than I could have done. To say I threw like a girl was an insult to every girl who ever lived. I even threw Frisbees sideways.

Tam didn't seem to be disappointed. In fact, Ben's halfway point appeared to be what he expected.

"Again," the goblin mage said. "Except this time, treat the rock as you would a stone of power." Tam's voice dropped into a lower register, soothing, hypnotic. I wondered if he didn't have a smidge of that spellsinger talent. "Hold it, reach out to it with your gift, then visualize the target and tell the rock the path you want it to take. Relax and take your time."

Ben closed his eyes and took a slow, deep breath. Then another, and yet another. When he opened his eyes, they were focused on the most distant target.

He threw the rock.

It shot from his hand and flew straight to the target, shattering the old whisky bottle perched on the peak of the boulder.

Dang.

Now *that* was a talent worth having. Color me jealous.

Ben was standing there with his mouth hanging open. "I did it."

Tam was smiling. "Of course, you did."

"What just happened here?" I asked. "Aside from the obvious, which was way cool."

"I suspected that Dr. Sadler's skills extended beyond stones of power to any rock or mineral," Tam said. "One of Agata's abilities involves using any rock as a weapon. She sees a target, relays that to any random rock she finds, and throws it. I've never seen her miss. Not to mention, seeing a Khrynsani get knocked out with a rock between the eyes is immensely satisfying." He glanced at Ben. "She can also call them back, so she only needs to carry a few."

Ian nodded in approval. "Reusable ammo. Nice."

"Would you care to call it back?" Tam asked Ben.

The gem mage had gone from dumbfounded to nearly giddy at the new trick he could so.

"Sure!"

"First you need to—"

Ben raised his mitt before Tam could finish.

If anything, the rock was moving faster on the return trip—and it was coming straight at us.

"Duck!" Ian shouted.

We all did.

Fortunately, the rock kept going. Unfortunately, it slammed into the Hummer's front bumper. The rock exploded into a bazillion pieces. The bumper didn't have a scratch.

Ben winced. "My bad."

17

Ben threw rocks and called them back under Tam's watchful eye until it was too dark to see the targets. After the first few, the rest of us went about our business, confident that Ben was past the whole "dangerous to himself and others" phase.

I took the opportunity to relax, or at least tried to.

Vacant buildings were popping out of existence all over the Southwest, each one larger than the building before. One, we barely knew who was responsible. Two, we had no clue what their evil masterplan was. However, we were fairly certain we were running out of time to stop number one from doing number two.

As far as we knew, Rake's house was the only building to be brought here from somewhere else. That somewhere else was another world. Every time I'd tried to wrap my mind around that I'd gotten a headache. It was one of those mind-expanding visuals of something you never expected to see, something that shouldn't be possible, but all too obviously was, rather like that deep space photo from the Hubble telescope. The one with the gazillon galaxies that was just a single, itty-bitty sliver of what was out there. The closer galaxies looked like galaxies. The ones farther away, like a single star. The mind-blowing part was that there were *so many.*

It was an astoundingly cool photo. So much so that I'd once made it my laptop wallpaper.

It'd lasted less than a day.

Why?

It freaked me the hell out.

That was the best way I could describe how looking at it made me feel. *Uneasy* didn't cover it, not by half. It made me feel small, insignificant, a speck of dust on a larger speck of dust, in a solar system in the middle of an average-sized galaxy spinning through what seemed like an endless universe. Did the universe end? If so, where? What did the end look like? Or was our universe a mere speck among a vast expanse of other universes, going on and on, never ending? Like that last shot in *Men in Black* that zoomed out from the galaxy-in-a-marble that Orion the cat had worn on his collar, to two gigantic aliens playing marbles with a whole bag full of them.

Like I said. Freaked. Out.

Tam said we needed to wait until it'd been full dark for at least an hour to give Ben the best chance for picking up a signal of the cabal's lair. The Khrynsani had gifted Isidor Silvanus with the equivalent of a bushel basket's worth of those crystals, and that was merely what Rake had managed to gather from his mind link. There could be more. It looked like we were going to catch a break and have a clear, cool night. Perfect for Ben's newfound crystal radar to do its thing.

Once we'd finished dinner, Rake let the fire die down to lessen any distractions for Ben. Rake, Tam, and Gethen were goblins with preternatural night vision. Between the wards, shields, and the guys, nothing or no one was sneaking up on us, so we mere mortals were free to enjoy the night sky.

Ian was doing just that. My partner was kicked back with a cold beer, slouched in his camp chair, head laid back, stargazing. I think it was the most relaxed I'd ever seen him.

He needed this. We all did.

I went about thirty feet outside of camp and turned away from the remains of the fire, gazing up into the night sky.

Without any cities nearby, the Milky Way was clearly visible. I'd been able to see the stars from the top of the mountain closest to home, but even then, there was light pollution from Knoxville. Aside from the ridge to our west, it was flat here, and the sky seemed to go on forever. Surprisingly, it didn't make me feel small. I felt as if I was part of something larger. There were advantages to getting away from civilization every now and then.

I sensed Rake coming up behind me.

"I can't wait to take you home," I told him. "October can't get here fast enough."

His arms went around my waist, pulling me back against him, his chin just above the top of my head.

"And I can't wait to go home with you," he murmured.

I smiled. "You might want to put your enthusiasm on hold until after you've met my family."

"I don't see that being a problem." He softly kissed the top of my head. "Are the stars as visible there?"

"Yes and no. If you go to the top of Widow's Peak, and the night is clear, you can see about…um, seventy percent of this. It just looks so much bigger here. I guess since you can see the horizon is why it looks like it goes on forever. I can definitely see why a sight like this is on a lot of peoples' bucket list."

"Bucket list?"

"Things people want to see before they kick the bucket, meaning die," I added before he could ask. I'd never realized how many idioms our language had; and when you were Southern, it tripled. "I don't plan on kicking any buckets anytime soon, but there's a lot of stuff I want to see."

Rake snuggled closer. "Anything you want."

I wiggled and turned in his arms so I was looking up into his eyes. I grinned. "Be careful how you throw those 'anythings' around. You might get more than you can handle."

"I can handle anything you need, want, or desire," he said in a husky whisper.

"This isn't nearly that acrobatic." I glanced back up at the sky. "Actually, it's quite simple, at least for you, Mr. Moneybags. First, I want to see the northern lights."

"That's it?"

"I said 'first.' Machu Picchu would be cool, so would Angkor Wat. I think I'd like to explore my own world, before I go traveling anywhere else." I tentatively pointed straight up. "You know, up there—where you're from."

Rake's solemn gaze searched my face. "I said 'anything' and I meant it."

"You've been wanting to spend money on me, so I might as well help you do it." My lips twitched at the corners. "On the way to Angkor Wat, those over-the-water huts on Bora Bora would be nice. I've always wanted to go there. I've got vacation time I haven't had time to take."

"It's about time you did."

"Tell me about it."

"You deserve it."

"And need it." I suddenly shivered—and not from cold.

Rake tightened his hold. "What is it?"

I unwrapped Rake's arms from around me. "Stay put." I instinctively kept my voice down. "And douse your magic for me."

He did. I quickly put about a dozen yards between us.

When I'd first moved to New York, I'd had a shiny new degree in journalism. The only job I'd been able to get was at a seedy tabloid called the *Informer* that specialized in the weird and spooky. My editor was a real creep, but it was easy to avoid him because of the cologne he marinated in every morning. I could smell where he'd been and where he was. That talent made me popular among the rest of the staff, who wanted to avoid him, too.

What I was getting now was still a scent, but a psychic one.

I'd sensed it in New York, and I sensed it now.

Marek Reigory.

"It's him," I said.

Rake came up beside me like a ghost, his magic held perfectly still.

I nodded toward the southern horizon where the faintest of glows was visible. "What's in that direction?"

Rake's smile was slow and dangerous. "Vegas, baby."

18

I wasn't the only one feeling the pull of Sin City.

Tam and Ben had gone even farther away from camp, and the two had returned with the same conclusion. Ben felt the pull of crystals from the south, and to the south was Las Vegas.

He'd also felt a crystal come-hither from the east, but it was vague, almost muffled. The signal from Vegas was definitely stronger. Since that was where I'd sensed Marek Reigory, that was where we were going.

Ian called headquarters to let Alain Moreau know where we were headed and why. He also told him about Ben's odd signal from the east and asked that he let Kenji know. Maybe it could help him pinpoint those missing buildings.

Mr. Moreau would arrange for yet another mode of transportation to take us to an airfield outside Las Vegas, where a car would be waiting. If Marek and any cabal members were expecting company, driving into town would be less likely to be noticed.

It was nearly ten o'clock when we broke camp to hit the road.

"Why can't the chopper pick us up here?" I asked as we loaded our gear into the Hummer.

"Terrain," Ian told me. "The only clear space is the town's street, and that's not wide enough. Everywhere else is too rocky." He grinned. "Unless you want to get reeled up a zipline."

"No thanks."

"Besides, we're ready to move now. By the time they get her fueled and prepped, we'll be where they are. The chopper will drop us off outside Vegas where the car will be waiting."

"To take us where in Vegas?" I asked.

Ian jerked his head toward Rake. "He's taking care of that part."

I turned to Rake. "To take us where in Vegas?"

"To a surprise." He thought for a moment and his lips twitched in a smile. "A strategic surprise."

Okaaay.

When we got underway, Gethen was driving because Rake was holding my hand. It wasn't for PDA purposes, but as insurance against Marek Reigory sensing me. We knew he was in Las Vegas and didn't want to send up a signal that we were coming for him. Rake was using a small magic to quiet any seer signals I might be sending out. We didn't want to risk Marek finding us before we found him.

"You've encountered him twice now," Rake was saying. "If he knows you've identified him, he'll be on the lookout for you."

"Would that be me personally, or just my seer senses?" I asked.

"It could be both. So, to be on the safe side, let's keep him from sensing either one."

"I wouldn't describe a psychic right hook and attempted immolation as encounters."

"It's a goblin thing." Gethen glanced in the rearview mirror at me as he bounced the Jeep across the desert. "In a violent confrontation, if no one dies, it's only an encounter."

I was in the backseat and Rake was in the front passenger seat. He had the seat pushed all the way back, so neither one of us had to contort to hold hands. The other reason why I wasn't driving was that it was pitch dark, there were no roads, and as a human, I couldn't see for squat. Ian had mapped our route to where the helicopter would be waiting to take us the hundred miles or so to the airfield outside Las Vegas.

I'd realized something—aside from the fact that a Jeep is a lot more fun if you're driving and freakin' miserable if you're bouncing around in the backseat. I could totally see a cabal of über evil mages setting up shop in Las Vegas. I mean, who would notice?

SPI's office in Las Vegas had less than a dozen agents and no commando team. When she'd expanded SPI's offices in the 1980s, Ms. Sagadraco had deemed that number sufficient to maintain ears to the wall and loafers on the ground. Our Los Angeles office was as fully staffed as our New York headquarters and was close enough to Vegas in case of an emergency. Las Vegas had a decent-sized supernatural population, most of them in the casinos and shows. Vampires made up the majority, and the mistress of the city did a fine job of keeping order in the ranks. She and Mr. Moreau were friends, and the boss trusted Cassandra du Vien to keep the peace.

All we knew so far was that Marek Reigory was in town with enough crystals to set off Ben's alarms. I was only a seer, but I had a sneaking suspicion we were gonna end up calling the LA folks or Madame du Vien for backup.

The helicopter waiting for us was large, black, and unless my sleep-deprived eyes deceived me, came complete with machine guns mounted on either side.

Cool. That is, unless Mr. Moreau thought we'd be needing them.

Ian noticed my apprehension. "We'll be flying into Nellis. This is one of their birds. SPI has contacts in all the military branches. We've scratched their backs, they scratch ours. Help when help is needed."

He didn't elaborate further, and to tell you the truth, the only thing I wanted to know about SPI and black helicopters was could I catch a few winks over the engine noise.

We got in and took off, and as far as I was concerned, we were flying way too low. It was pretty much all desert below us, but I still thought we were entirely too close to it.

"This feels like dragon flight, but without the wind in your face," Tam told us. "My team and I flew from the coast of Aquas inland to Nidaar on battle dragons that were about this size."

"How long did it take to get there?" I asked.

"We left at sunset and arrived shortly after sunrise."

Ben gave a low, impressed whistle.

Flying all night. In the open air. I couldn't even begin to imagine. Nor did I want to.

Tam admired the gun outside the window. "Our dragons could breathe fire."

"A Black Hawk can breathe Hellfire missiles," Ian told him.

"Sounds impressive. What are—"

"Basically, a tube packed with explosives with a range of almost five miles."

"That would be better than dragon fire," Tam admitted, then his fangs flashed in a quick grin, "but not nearly as much fun."

"I've never flown a dragon, but I think I'd have to agree with you."

"If you visit our world, I could make arrangements."

Now it was Ian's turn to grin. "I just might take you up on that."

I just stood there and stared. "*This* is Moreau's idea of inconspicuous?"

Our ride into town was a limo so sleek and so black I could see myself in the paint job.

"I couldn't have made a better choice myself," Rake said. "Think about it. It's just after midnight in Las Vegas. No one will look twice at us. And if they try, the windows are tinted as dark as the rest of the car." He waggled his eyebrows at me. "Complete privacy."

"Yeah, if there weren't four guys in the back with us."

Rake leaned in close, his lips at my ear. "My surprise later will remedy the privacy issue."

"You keep promising surprises. I've told you I don't like those, right?"

"You've made that abundantly clear on multiple occasions. I consider it a personal challenge to shower you with so many breathtaking surprises that you'll come to love them."

"You say 'breathtaking' like it's a good thing."

He nipped my earlobe with his fangs. "Have I ever taken your breath in a bad way?"

A shiver ran to all my favorite places. "No, you certainly have not. Touché."

Rake gave a wicked chuckle. "Touché? I plan to."

19

Rake's idea of a strategic surprise was the Nobu Villa in the Nobu Hotel at Caesars Palace. We needed to keep a low profile. Rake didn't do low profiles, at least not of his own free will. Though when you paid what he had to have paid for this place, all the privacy you wanted must have been included in the tab.

I was in a shocked stupor as I tried to take it all in.

I had no words.

Rake had plenty. "It's what we need. It's near the center of the Strip with views north and south." He threw open two humongous glass doors leading out onto a terrace that was bigger than the bullpen at SPI HQ.

My jaw dropped farther.

"Plus, the rooftop terrace will give you and Ben

unobstructed, upper floor, open-air access to the Vegas sky. Marek is here, and you'll find him."

Ian gave me a nudge and showed me his phone's screen. He'd Googled where we were. He scrolled and I scanned. A 10,500-square-foot, three-bedroom villa with two butlers, and a 4,700-square-foot terrace, all for the low, low price of $35,000 a night.

Sweet mother of God.

"It kind of reminds me of the suite from *The Hangover*," Ian murmured with a boyish grin seldom seen on my partner. "Only bigger."

"But without the wandering chicken," I noted.

"And, thankfully, without the tiger in the bathroom," Ben muttered.

I gave a quiet snort. "This is Rake we're talking about. You might want to check the bathrooms first."

Rake ignored us and continued, clearly proud of his choice. "We're at about the midpoint on the Strip, and we're high enough to give you and Ben a clear shot at whatever signals there are to pick up, and private enough to keep our presence here a secret until we're ready to kick in Marek's door." With a flourish, he threw open the doors to the dining room. "And regardless of the hour, the chefs at Nobu downstairs are at our beck and call. Sushi. anyone?"

We all passed on the sushi, opting instead to wash off the desert dust and get to work.

I got a shower in a bathroom that was bigger than my entire apartment, and gave a longing little whimper at a bathtub I could've done laps in. The mother of all soaks would have to wait.

I had a megalomaniacal goblin mage to find.

It was coming up on two o'clock in the morning. Marek Reigory was a goblin, goblins were nocturnal, and Las Vegas slept even less than New York.

There wasn't going to be a better time to find him.

After my shower, I got dressed in the only extra clothes I'd brought with me: jeans and a henley. I'd done my best to knock the desert dust off my hiking boots. I didn't think any of us had imagined that we'd end up in Vegas, and definitely not in the Grand Poobah Suite. Well, except for Rake. He was kind of like a goblin James Bond in that respect, and a few others besides. The only luggage he'd brought was a small duffel bag, but I wouldn't be surprised if he had a tux rolled up in there. Just in case. Or since he was a mage, maybe the duffel had a direct link to his closets in New York. Kind of like Mary Poppins's carpet bag.

After a couple of wrong turns, I found my way out of the master bedroom and to the living room, or whatever it was called here. Everyone else had already gathered. I detected the scent of newly worked magic. Rake and Tam had put a ward on the penthouse similar to what they'd done to our campsite.

"I take it you've fixed it so any mages in town think this place is empty?" I asked Rake.

"Au contraire, it is occupied, just not by us. Tam and I went with a more mundane disguise, one that would be expected for Las Vegas. Should any mage come snooping, this villa is occupied by a group of rich twenty- and thirtysomethings here for a couple of days that they won't be able to remember next week."

"'Mundane' meaning there's no livestock or jungle cats," added a freshly shampooed Ben from the sofa. He'd been the first to pass on the sushi, but he'd apparently hit the fully stocked bar. I didn't know what he was drinking, but I smelled coconut and wanted one.

Work now, Mac. Drink later.

"You wanna go first?" I asked him.

Ben raised his glass. "I've already been. This is my celebratory drink."

"You hit pay dirt?"

"For Vegas, more like 'jackpot.' No real work necessary. I just opened my senses, and there they were. All we need now is your confirmation."

I grunted. "No pressure. How many crystals are here?"

"A lot. I couldn't determine the exact number, but the signal was magnitudes stronger than I got from the ones back at headquarters."

"They weren't warded?"

Ben shook his head. "The crystals weren't. Reigory might be."

"It seems Marek doesn't know we're on to him yet," Rake said. "Or if he knows, that knowledge doesn't concern him."

"Let's hope for door number one," I told him. "Did you open the ward for Ben?"

"For about ten seconds."

I headed for the terrace. "Let's see if I can beat his time."

20

Rake silently followed me outside.

The noise hit me the instant I opened the terrace doors. You'd think it'd be quiet at two o'clock in the morning, but in Las Vegas, it was prime partying time. The Nobu Hotel had plexiglass mounted around the edges of the terrace to above head level to keep drunken guests from taking an inadvertent swan dive into whatever was below. I had no intention of looking down to find out.

Our villa was far from the highest hotel room in town, but Rake was right, it provided an excellent view both up and down the Strip. Most important for our purposes, it was open-air.

I went to the corner of the terrace with the best view.

Just down from Caesars Palace was the Bellagio with its giant marquee out front advertising its Cirque du Soleil show.

As I said, Las Vegas was a vampire town; not surprising, really. It woke up at night, and the Cirque du Soleil shows in hotels up and down the Strip used vampires' preternatural grace and beauty to the max. People had always been amazed at how humans could move, contort, or balance like that. There were a few mortals among the casts, and a sprinkling of other supernaturals, but most were vampires. They made a killing in this town, so to speak.

Rake stopped a few feet behind me. "I'll move the ward back just enough to leave you exposed."

"Gee, you make that sound safe."

"It's not, and I don't like it."

"I get that impression."

"This is no joke. He's dangerous, Makenna."

"I got that impression, too."

"Work fast. The ward is right behind you. If he senses you, just take one step back, and you'll be safe. And if he tries anything, I'm here—and the gloves come off."

I gave a single nod and focused my seer senses on the Strip. Rake smoothly pulled the ward back, and I was suddenly alone as if he and the others no longer existed.

Normally, I'd close my eyes for what I was about to do. Not here and not now. I relaxed as best as I could and simply went still, opening my senses to the psychic scent I'd come to know as Marek Reigory. If he had shielded himself like Rake and Tam had protected us, I either wouldn't be able to sense him at all, or getting a fix on his location would be tricky at best, unless he…

There.

I swallowed a squeak, and all but fell back through the ward.

Rake didn't ask if I'd found him, it was obvious that I had. He quickly pushed the ward back against the plexiglass. "He's close?"

"Very." I shuddered from head to toe, just like I had in the desert, but it was worse this time. I gave a weak laugh. "Who needs to use seer senses? I just need to wait for a big ol' wave of the heebie-jeebies." I shuddered again.

"Did he sense you?"

"I don't think so." I thought for a moment. "No. No, he didn't."

Rake stepped up to the glass, his eyes intent on the Strip below. "Where is he?"

I nodded toward the north, beyond the Bellagio next door. "That way."

"Distance?"

"Less than a mile."

"That's what Ben said. That means Marek's staying with the crystals. Good."

My shivers finally stopped. "One-stop shopping," I managed.

"Just the way I like it. Do you have a fix on him?"

"Oh yeah."

Rake flashed a predatory smile. "Let's take a drive down the Strip and do a little sightseeing."

I thought Rake and I and maybe Gethen would go.

Silly me.

There was no way Ian was letting me go anywhere without him. Ben wanted to double-check his own findings, and apparently when Tam had retired from being a royal magical enforcer, he'd gone into the nightclub and casino business back home, and now owned several. Tam wanted to see more, more, more of Las Vegas.

Thankfully, the limo and driver were available. I guess when you dropped thirty-five grand a night on a hotel room, the amenities just kept coming.

It was Friday night—actually, Saturday morning—and the Strip was nearly bumper-to-bumper. Mr. Moreau had been right about a limo being inconspicuous. As we headed north, nearly a fourth of the vehicles cruising the Strip were limos. There was one aspect that made ours stand out like a sore thumb. We were one of the few without people in various stages of inebriation standing up through the sunroof or hanging out the windows and waving an assortment of bottles, glasses, or red Solo cups. And from what my ears were telling me, the near universal vocalization was "Wooooo!" It was a good thing our windows were up and tinted, though. If the bachelorette party in the limo next to us had gotten a gander of the guys I was riding around with…

"Are we shielded?" Ben was asking.

"As soon as we got in," Rake assured him. "If Marek knows we're here, all he'll get from this limo is six friends on their way back to their hotel, too drunk to stand up through the sunroof."

"Works for me."

"We're getting closer," I told them. "It's just on the other side of the next hotel on the right. Ben?"

"That's what I got."

Beside that hotel was another hotel.

The Phoenix.

It was smaller than the glass-towered properties on either side of it, but in my opinion, it had more panache. It wasn't an old hotel, but it had been designed to look like an updated version of a classic Vegas hotel from the 1960s.

My attention went to the hotel's marquee. It was a masterpiece of neon art. A red Phoenix spread its wings and arose from flames that climbed and licked the night sky like real fire. After launching itself into flight, the Phoenix folded its wings, succumbing to the flames, and was consumed. It was born and died again and again.

"That's almost as cool as the fountains," Ben said.

I couldn't have agreed more.

Below the fire was a marquee with the hotel's name in stylized script that alternated with advertisements of the hotel's show, complete with a larger-than-life, up-close video snippet of the headliner.

A classically tall, dark, and handsome man all in black. Dark, smoldering eyes gave every passerby on the Strip an irresistible come-hither.

With fangs. Visible for all to see.

A vampire hiding in plain sight as a human pretending to be a vampire.

I did a double take, and not because he was hot.

He wasn't a vampire. He was a goblin.

Marek Reigory.

In addition to tight black leather, he was wearing one of the most incredibly thorough glamours I'd ever seen. Even though it was video, I could just make out the goblin beneath.

Marek Reigory was working in a Las Vegas hotel as a magician named Keram Rei.

A hotel that, according to the next screen on the marquee, he was going to make disappear tomorrow night in a sold-out show.

21

The marquee quickly went on to advertise the hotel's all-you-can-eat buffet.

I think I was the only one who'd seen the digital portent of doom. In the guys' defense, there was an awful lot to look at. Aside from the neon lightshow, the bachelorettes were still woooo'ing from the limo next door, and the bride had just whipped off her top and was swinging it around her head.

"Uh…guys," I managed. "We need to call the boss. Now."

Ian leaned forward to get a better look when the video rotated back to the show after a promo of half-price drinks at the pool bar from noon to two. "Is that who I think—"

"You better believe it," I told him.

"Oh, my God," Ben breathed in the brief, but total, silence that followed. "He's going to make the hotel…and it's sold out. All those people…"

Rake's words that followed did not call on any god, goblin or human. They were all directed at Marek Reigory. Ian made a one-word contribution to Rake's profoundly profane linguistic litany, and then he had his phone out, calling Alain Moreau.

"His alias is 'Marek' spelled backward, with the first three letters of his last name," Tam noted. "He's playing with us."

Rake snarled as he reached for his own phone. "Playtime's over."

Only in Las Vegas could you advertise that you were going to make a building disappear and people would stand in line to buy tickets to be inside when it happened.

Marek had named his show "The Phoenix Illusion," except the hotel vanishing with thousands of innocent people inside wouldn't be an illusion, and the disappearance of those thousands would be all too real.

I wasn't the only one thinking along those lines.

"Who would want to be inside a building that's going to disappear?" Ben was asking. We were back in the suite, which Ian and Rake were rapidly turning into a war room. "Just what do they think is going to happen to them? The building vanishes, and they're left sitting in an empty lot?"

I had my tablet out, searching online for everything I could find on Keram Rei and his show. Kenji would dig up much more. While we were on our way back from the Phoenix, I'd called him and told him what we needed. It'd been a little after two o'clock in the morning, which would've made it a little after five in New York. Kenji had been groggy when he'd answered the phone, but once I filled him in on the evil who, what, when, where, and why of our dire situation, our elf tech guru was instantly Mountain Dew-level awake.

It was now closing in on four o'clock, but before our room service breakfast arrived in two hours, I was sure Kenji would have sent us only the first wave of every down and dirty detail there was to know about Marek Reigory's magician alias. If it could be had, Kenji would dig it out and serve it up.

"It says here a local network affiliate will have cameras set up outside the Phoenix tonight to record what happens," I told Ben. "At least the TV people have enough sense to stay outside."

After Ian had called HQ to report our findings, I had no doubt Vivienne Sagadraco would be coming into the office.

She kept a more or less human schedule and worked during the day. Mr. Moreau ruled the night shift at SPI. Only when a situation merited an all-hands emergency designation did Ms. Sagadraco work round the clock.

I'd be stunned if Mr. Moreau wasn't giving the boss lady a wakeup call right now.

Marek Reigory was going to take a hotel from the middle of the Vegas Strip, with thousands of people inside, and send it to an unknown location either here or in another dimension, or maybe even another world. If that didn't qualify as an all-hands event back home, I didn't know what would.

I Googled for any mention of the hotel or Marek's show.

I found that the hotel had been built five years ago, so it'd only been designed to look like something from the '60s. It was a boutique hotel, its smaller size an effort to get back to the glamorous Las Vegas of the Rat Pack, before dancing

musical fountains, gondolas, erupting volcanos, shark aqua-
riums, replicas of cities and the like took over the Strip. While
it was dwarfed by the resorts around it, what it lacked in
square footage, it more than made up for in attracting A-listers
from Hollywood, and two of the hottest celebrity chefs for its
two restaurants. Its casino wasn't the dark, smoke-filled maze
with gaudy carpet to hide the stains from spilled drinks. It was
named the Golden Egg, in reference to the goose that laid the
Golden Egg, and maybe in keeping with the whole bird motif.
The casino looked like how middle America expected casinos
to look from the movies. Elegant and Monte Carlo-ish with a
strict dress code. Men in tuxedos or suits, women in evening
gowns or cocktail dresses, like something out of a James Bond
or Humphrey Bogart movie. No tourists in Bermuda shorts,
Hawaiian shirts, and sandals with black socks. It wasn't
allowed there, and it shouldn't be allowed anywhere. There
were standards, tasteful standards. Quite frankly, if I were to
have a hotel and casino here, I'd want it to be like the Phoenix.

"Who owns the Phoenix?" I asked.

Gethen jerked his head toward where Rake paced in the
hall, phone attached to his ear. "He's on it."

Next, I found an article about last night's show. "This
is interesting," I said to Ben and anyone else who might be
listening. "In the last two shows, I guess as a warmup for
tonight, Marek made himself disappear from the stage and then
reappear at a nightclub at the hotel next door. Naturally, there
were TV cameras waiting. After that, there was essentially a
stampede at the Phoenix box office to buy the few remaining
tickets."

Attached was a video of Marek popping into view in the

middle of the club's dance floor, scaring the bejesus out of some older tourists badly gettin' their groove on. I noticed he was wearing the same cuff with a glowing green crystal that he'd used to escape when he attacked me.

Tam looked over my shoulder. "It's Sythsaurian technology. We took a few of those cuffs from some dead Khrynsani in Nidaar. They're still being studied to determine how they work. It appears that's how Marek plans to escape once he activates that crystal. Those last two shows were tests for his escape."

I watched the video again, looking for anything that could help us.

When he'd attacked me, Marek had only been wearing one cuff. Now he was wearing one on each wrist.

"He's wearing two now. Does he need both?" I asked Tam.

"I don't see why he would. Though if I was depending on one of those cuffs to escape a hotel about to be ripped from reality, I'd want a backup. I'll be willing to bet Marek won't do his illusion if he's not wearing them."

"It'd be like robbing a bank without a getaway car," I said.

Ian came into the room and dropped his phone in his shirt pocket. "More like setting a bomb to go off with no way out."

Ben had scooted over next to me on the couch and was reading the article that went along with the video. "He has a lot of people believing he's a vampire, which I think would really piss off the real thing."

I snorted. "Talk about cultural appropriation."

Rake came back into the room. "I can't see Marek doing this without high-powered mage security," he told

Ian. "Probably Khrynsani. He'd want his own people. This has been planned for a long time, with at least six months of testing."

"There'll be wards out the wazoo," I muttered. "Nasty ones."

"By the way," Rake continued, "the Phoenix is owned by Laerin Asset Management."

Tam barked a laugh.

I looked back and forth between the two goblins. "What?"

"Laerin is a city in Pengor, which is the elven kingdom," Tam told me. "The Silvanus family controls Laerin. It's the center of their financial and political empire—though a more accurate description would be their criminal empire."

Rake and Gethen exchanged a glance.

Ian gave them a flat look. "You boys care to share with the rest of the class?"

"Lady Makenna, can you find if any of his major shows have been broadcast?" Gethen asked.

"Check YouTube," Ben suggested. "Somebody had to have snuck a phone recording."

Rake nodded. "We're looking for any VIPs. Pay close attention to anyone seated near the stage. They'll probably look bored, as if they've been there, seen that. More than likely they'll be glamoured."

I sighed, as much for myself as for Ian. "For once, can you just tell us what's going on in your head *first, then* make with the cryptic requests?"

"Marek likes what he considers to be a fun scheme as much as the next Bond villain wannabe," Rake said, "but this is too big for him—at least too big for him to plan and execute by himself. I'm not saying he's not qualified to do it. He is. This is simply beyond what Marek would *want* to take on by himself. As far as he's concerned, too many boring details equals not enough fun."

I blinked. "He's a *lazy* Bond villain?"

"He merely prefers to work alone. He has trust issues, especially with non-goblins. There's entirely too much planning, timing, and coordination involved here for Marek to enjoy himself. And unless he has to, Marek doesn't do anything he doesn't enjoy. He seems to be the centerpiece of this operation, at least the one in the spotlight. *That* is the part he would enjoy. In New York, you said he was angry and anxious."

"Yes."

"That's the part he hates—having to depend on others not to screw up. I've been thinking about it, and with my house, somebody definitely screwed up. I don't think it was supposed to have been taken at all, or if it was, it wasn't supposed to have been dropped in the middle of New York. Though if that hadn't happened, we probably wouldn't have been on to this at all, or not until it was too late. All that means Marek has accomplices—and people who he's reporting to. Furthermore, mages at his level of power and above have ego issues—"

I was all innocence. "You don't say?"

"This is an important operation to whoever is ultimately in charge," Rake continued, ignoring my jab without missing a beat. "Marek screwed up in New York. Even though it wasn't him personally, it was someone he was responsible for. He's being watched by his higher-ups in this cabal, or whatever it is they call themselves. If they were at either of the past two nights' shows, which is probable since his disappearance was a test for his escape tonight, the most likely place for them would be in any VIP seating—front row, front table, or a box if the Phoenix's theater has them."

"There might also have been someone waiting in the nightclub at the hotel next door," I suggested as I reached for my phone. "I'll have Kenji see if he can hack into both hotels' security videos. He's been working on a facial recognition program that lets him review tape at any speed and the program will stop it when it IDs anyone on our most-watched or wanted lists. That is, if they're not glamoured. He hasn't figured out a way to do that yet."

Ian gave me a nod of approval. "Good thinking, partner."

"Yes, very good," Rake added. "We'll need you to review the VIP sections to determine if any of them are using glamours. Marek's own ego won't let him answer to anyone he considers to be less powerful than himself. That makes it even more likely that those in charge occupy places of dishonor on both of Vivienne's lists. It's critical that we know who we're going up against. More lives are at stake than just tonight's audience."

No pressure.

22

After all that, I still managed a yawn. Nearly hourly bursts of adrenaline would wear anybody out.

"Why don't you try to get some sleep, darling?" Rake suggested. "We've got a big day ahead of us, and you haven't slept in…"

I did some groggy calculations, but couldn't come up with a number. "I can't remember."

"You need to be alert," Ian said. "Go get some sleep."

"Kenji will be calling me back."

"Leave me your phone. I'll take care of it."

"What about you? You've been awake just as long as I have. When are you gonna sleep?"

"I'll grab a power nap."

With his background, Ian could probably go to infinity

and beyond without sleep. I couldn't go to infinity, let alone beyond. Heck, right now, I didn't even think I could spell it.

Nighty-night time it was.

I kept regular daylight office hours at SPI. Usually. Unless something big was going down, then I went until I couldn't go any more. The forces of evil didn't clock in and out, so neither could I.

My problem was that when I was borderline exhausted, more often than not, exhaustion brought along her good friend insomnia.

Insomnia was a jerk.

In addition, my subconscious had brought paranoia, fear, and inadequacy to the sleepover.

I did meditative breathing. No go. I tried counting sheep, but just as I was starting to doze off, the fluffy little sheep turned into zombie sheep and attacked me.

Rake came in and quietly closed the door behind him. "Can't sleep?"

"Let's see… Unless we stop him, a crazy goblin mage—no insult intended—"

Rake crossed the room to the bed. "None taken. I'm not crazy."

"Is going to snuff an entire hotel out of existence, possibly killing thousands of people—"

Rake slid into the bed next to me.

"On TV, in the most public outing of supernatural power since the boss's sister tried to turn a herd of grendels loose in Times Square on New Year's—"

"Shhh." Rake's lips descended onto mine.

"Relaxing isn't happening." At least that's what I tried to say, but it got muffled.

"That's what I thought." Rake's arms went around me and gently pulled me close. The rest of him got even closer. His voice was a husky whisper. "I'm here to help."

"I got that feeling." And Rake's knee sliding between my legs was giving me even more feelings.

"I put too much pressure on you." His lips hovered just above mine. "That was wrong, and I'm sorry."

"No, you were right. It's what I was hired to do." I went silent for a few moments. "It's just that…I feel like a third-string Little Leaguer told they have to pitch in the final game of the World Series."

Rake pulled back, his brow creased in confusion. "I don't know what some of that means."

"You're kidding? You live in New York and—"

"Shhh." Another lingering kiss.

"It's a sports analogy," I managed when I came up for air.

"I don't care about sports," he whispered against my lips, followed by another kiss, this time deeper.

As Rake's lips started to wander south, I found I didn't care, either. And when his hands joined the journey, I forgot what baseball was, except for the overwhelming need to round third base for a home run.

I woke up in a little pool of drool.

The clock beside the bed said 7:55.

I'd slept nearly four hours, but Vegas probably hadn't even blinked.

The side of the bed next to me had been slept in, but not

for long. I wasn't surprised. Marek was a couple of hotels down the Strip plotting evil of apocalyptic proportions. His show started at nine o'clock tonight. We had thirteen hours. Hopefully that would be lucky thirteen. Rake and Ian were plotting how to stop him in his tracks. I knew full well Rake was anticipating going beyond that and had probably kept himself awake with entertaining scenes of murder and mayhem that would make his previous blood-soaked encounter with Marek look like a pillow fight.

I grabbed another shower, got dressed, and left the master suite in search of breakfast.

There was still plenty of food left on the sideboard in the dining room. Rake had ordered enough to feed a small army, but the guys had already put a respectable dint in the provisions. I got myself a plate and vowed to do my part to put a serious hurtin' on what was left.

I sat down to eat, but within a few minutes I heard voices raised in debate from the terrace. I took my plate, refilled my humongous cup of coffee, and joined them.

"This is the first time," Ian was saying, "—that we know of—when people will be in a building that's going to be taken."

"Aside from Tulis in my house," Rake reminded him.

"And look how that turned out." Ian spread his hands. "Boom. Followed by it burning to the ground."

"It blew up and burned *when it landed,*" Ben pointed out. "That could have been because it came from…outer space." He looked to Rake. "Is that offensive?"

"What?"

"Saying it came from outer space?"

Rake and Tam exchanged confused glances. "Why would it be?"

"It implies you guys are aliens."

"Are we?" Tam asked Rake.

"We are," Rake told him.

Tam shrugged. "I'm not offended."

"Me, either."

"Good," Ben said brightly. "We have no idea where they're planning to send the Phoenix—here or somewhere else."

"Kenji's using satellites to look around the southwest for the cabal's headquarters," Ian said. "We're thinking they may have brought the buildings there. I told him about you sensing a muffled crystal signal from the east of Shiloh City."

"I don't want to be the voice of doom," Tam said, "but what if the only reason Tulis survived was because he's a mage and was able to shield and protect himself?"

There was silence at that pronouncement.

"We don't know that there haven't been people in the buildings that were taken," Ian said.

I stopped chewing. "All of them were out in the middle of nowhere. Chances are they were empty."

"But we have no proof they were empty. It would hardly be the first time people have been used as guinea pigs in the sick experiments of others."

Rake came over and sat on the sofa next to me. "Griselda Ingeborg, one of the mages on SPI's list with Marek, once kidnapped homeless people to test a…magical hypothesis. I would rather not describe the hypothesis, her tests, or the results, but I heard the people she'd kidnapped did not survive."

Tam poured himself another cup of coffee from the carafe on the table. "That Marek and his accomplices have stopped secret testing in favor of public action implies they either don't plan on those in the hotel surviving, or they have the means to keep them prisoner in the hotel once the building is taken. My bet is on the latter scenario."

The rest of us, except for Ben, traded startled looks of realization. Ben was the only one of us who hadn't been trapped in the Regor Regency.

Phaeon had used his first-generation magetech generator to seal hundreds of us, many of whom were powerful magic users, inside the Regor Regency. Isidor had conjured a pocket dimension around the hotel to keep us there.

"*We* were the people test," I blurted. "There were only a couple hundred of us trapped inside, but most of the guests were either supernaturals or powerhouse mages—and we *still* couldn't get out." Another lightbulb went on in my head. "Because the generator affected everyone's magic." I turned to Rake. "Like what happened when your shields failed when you ran into your house to go after Tulis. There'll be thousands in the Phoenix tonight, but they're only human. Power-wise, it'll be like scooping up a litter of newborn kittens."

"But the Regor Regency wasn't taken anywhere," Ian pointed out. "And it was only a month ago. Kenji said the buildings started disappearing over *six* months ago."

I spat a word that as a kid would've gotten my mouth washed out with soap. "You're right." I took another big ol' swig of coffee.

"Don't give up on your theory just yet," Rake said. "The cube and a Nidaar crystal are not only different in composition, but in what they are being used to do. The cube sealed us in a pocket dimension and powered the mirrors and reflective surfaces to let monsters pass through into the Regency. The Nidaar crystal is mounted in a device that may or may not be the same as that which Marek is using. Yes, Dr. Cheban determined that the *casing* was constructed of the same metal, but that doesn't mean what's inside is the same. Isidor and Phaeon wanted to trap us and send in monsters to finish us off, and that included the leaders of the supernatural races on this world. Their goal was to decimate the races, destroy SPI's position as an arbiter of supernatural peace, and humiliate me and ruin my reputation and honor as a host who failed to protect my guests." He paused. "And then kill me slowly and horribly."

"They appear to be using the Nidaar crystal only to move buildings," Gethen said.

"And those inside them," Tam added. "I fail to see the strategic advantage in taking a building in a way that would kill those inside. Thinking as our opposition, it would be an incredibly efficient way to kidnap powerful individuals, or even better, *many* powerful individuals. You wouldn't need to get anywhere near them, merely get the device and crystal in the same building. Entire governments could be decimated in one fell swoop."

"Which is why we need to catch the bastards now," Gethen said.

"Which begs the question of why they would take a Las Vegas hotel full of tourists?" Ben asked. "Why not a building with really important people inside?"

I glanced at Ian. "We need a list of people in tonight's audience."

"Kenji," we said in unison.

"And speaking of our source of all unattainable knowledge," I continued, "Kenji says that while the entire southwest is a nest of ley lines and energy vortexes, it just so happens a massive ley line runs right down the Vegas Strip."

"That's why Las Vegas was built here," Rake said. "Luck is perceived as being higher near ley lines. Otherwise, why build hotels out in the middle of the desert?"

"That makes sense," I admitted, talking fast after nearly two colossal cups of coffee. "As to why here, maybe for their first strike, they're going for instilling terror rather than for any strategic importance. It'll be Saturday night in the middle of the Vegas Strip. A hotel vanishes, leaving a ginormous vacant lot. The power will go out up and down the Strip. There'll be glowing gold swirls in the sky. People will panic. Complete chaos. And when the lights *do* come on, the Phoenix will be gone. The cabal then sends whatever demands they have to the media; or heck, they just tweet out a video of imprisoned and terrified people freaking out in the hotel, with the 'you're next if you don't give us what we want' spiel. Or even worse, 'we're mages with magic and technology you can't hope to match. Kneel before your new overlords.'"

Silence followed my torrent of caffeinated words.

"I really need some more sleep," I said.

"You may need more sleep," Rake said, "but either of those scenarios is entirely too plausible. However, the last one would be worse."

"If they succeed, I have no doubt they'll tell us their demands," Ian said. "I'd rather stop Marek now, bring him in, and—in a locked interrogation room with no cameras—find out *exactly* what the cabal is planning."

Rake gave my partner a fierce grin. "Sounds like the man has a plan. I like it."

23

There was a knock on the door.

It couldn't be the butlers; Rake had turned down their services, instead preferring the comfort of walking around the suite unglamoured.

"Expecting anyone?" I asked Rake.

At the moment of the knock, he and Tam had simultaneously uncoiled from their chairs in a single smooth move. Ian and Gethen were on their feet an instant later. Ian had a gun in his hand; Gethen was packing a red glow. Rake and Tam had no visible weapons, apparently counting on their innate badassery to deal with whatever was on the other side of the door.

I tossed a questioning glance at Ben. He shrugged. We followed.

By the time we got there, the door was open, and Ian had been engulfed by a huge, hairy whatever, and the goblins weren't doing a thing to help.

Ben took a step back. "Is that a sasquat—"

"Yasha!" I squealed happily. A petite silvery-haired woman stepped around him. "Kitty!"

At the sound of my voice, Yasha tossed Ian aside, and I was now the target of his enthusiasm. Fortunately, I remembered to suck in all the air I could before my feet left the floor.

Before my face was buried in his chest fur, I saw my friend was the embodiment of Vegas tourist chic: Hawaiian shirt, cargo shorts, straw fedora, and Oakleys. Instead of the dreaded socks 'n sandals combo, in true Yasha fashion, my werewolf buddy was sporting his favorite combat boots.

Take that fashion risk, Yasha. Own it.

When he put me down, I saw the fanny pack. I knew what had to be in there. One of his guns. As a werewolf, it wasn't like Yasha needed protection. He just liked things that went boom.

As far as I was concerned, Ian was only one of my partners. Yasha was the other. Ian had my back, but Yasha had both our backs and then some. And the last time we'd dealt with a situation that could only be explained with physics that hurt my head, Kitty had been there to shut it down.

We had the goblin spellslinger trio for Marek and his gang, Ben for the rocks, Kitty for the sciencey woo-woo, and Yasha to kick any and all butts that deserved it.

The team was together.

We might actually live through this.

After we brought Yasha and Kitty up to speed, we got them fed.

Kitty looked from Rake to Tam as the two of us sat at the kitchen bar while she had breakfast. "Are you sure they're not brothers?" she barely whispered.

"Quite," they said in unison from across the room.

Kitty emitted a little giggle. "Oops."

"Goblin ears, sweetie," I reminded her. "They're good for something besides nibbling on."

Ben was working on a bagel, and Ian was stalwartly keeping Yasha company as both men laid into the breakfast buffet. Or maybe it was emotional support. I suspected that Rake was gonna need to have the sideboard restocked. My partners were serious when it came to fueling up for a fight, and all of us knew that's exactly what we were going to have on our hands tonight.

Kitty shook her head in affectionate disbelief. "He nearly ate my parents out of house and home. Mom was in heaven. There's nothing she loves more than feeding people who love her cooking. Though they knew I was bringing a werewolf home a week before a full moon. He's even hungrier than usual."

"Yeah, he is *really* hairy right now, isn't he? How did it go with your folks?"

Kitty beamed. "They absolutely adore him. Dad's a big guy and gun nut, too, so he and Yasha had a lot in common. They took a case of beer and I don't know how many guns and boxes of ammo out to Dad's firing range. From the sounds of things, Mom and I knew they were either having a great time or killing each other repeatedly."

"And the whole werewolf thing didn't bother them?"

"Not at all. My family has been portalkeepers for too many generations to count. We open and close portals to other worlds and dimensions. I only brought home a man who gets hairier once a month. Well, and then there's the fangs. But in my family, Yasha's what's known as a refreshing change."

"Wish me luck next month with Rake and my family. And extended family," I muttered.

"You don't think they'll like him?"

"I think they will, but I'm gonna be eating Tums like candy to get through it."

"From what you've told me of your family, I think you'll be surprised."

"That's the one kind of surprise I'd actually like to get."

Gethen and Tam were reviewing the most recent Keram Rei performance that'd been broadcast. It'd actually been on one of those magician specials on cable.

"I've seen his shows on TV, and last year live in Chicago," Kitty was saying. "Now, I'm ashamed to say that I enjoyed them." She lowered her voice nearly to the point of just moving her lips. "He's hot."

I couldn't tell her she was wrong. What was wrong was that I agreed with her. Just because a guy was evil didn't mean he couldn't be seriously easy on the eyes. Some of the most beautiful predators were the most deadly.

"He's well known," Kitty continued. "I wouldn't consider him famous, but he's getting there. Yeah, he projects the whole bad boy image, but his shows are fun, too. Though knowing now what he plans to do…" She took a swig of juice. "I mean, who would believe it? It'd be like Penn and Teller going to the dark side."

"Did he make anything big disappear in Chicago?" I asked.

Kitty shook her head. "But then he didn't have access to an alien crystal, ley line power, and a super blue blood moon tonight. If Yasha didn't have such good control—"

"A what?"

"Yasha would be all-out furry if—"

"Not Yasha, the moon."

"It's a super blue blood moon tonight."

"I thought that was next week."

"No, it's tonight."

I turned on my swivel bar stool. "Uh, guys…"

Turned out everyone knew it was a super blue blood moon tonight except for me.

That didn't make me feel stupid. Not at all.

"Marek probably couldn't make it work at any other time," Kitty was saying. "He needs the power boost from that supermoon. Timing is everything. They've been planning this for a long time. To move a building full of people will take as much power as they can harness. The amount needed will be nothing short of staggering."

"So, there's no way Marek is doing this by himself?" Ian asked.

"Absolutely not." Kitty held up a hand. "That's only my opinion."

"An *expert* opinion," Ian countered. "One I am inclined to accept as fact."

"Aww, thank you, Ian."

That opinion came from a woman who'd once closed a portal linking Hell and Earth, *with* demons scrabbling up through it. Yes, Rake had been there with her, but he'd been acting more as an emotional support goblin than providing any actual assistance. Kitty had done the heavy lifting all by her lonesome.

That Kitty was awestruck by the power involved told us there was absolutely nothing good about our situation, considering that we had only hours to stop Marek Reigory and whoever comprised *his* support team, and to get that generator and all crystals away from them without any mortal in the Phoenix Hotel or cruising the Strip tonight being any the wiser.

We'd be needing every bit of the luck Vegas's ley line could be sweet-talked into giving us.

"The barriers between dimensions and worlds are thinner during these conditions," Kitty was telling everyone. "They're not using a portal, but if you were going to pull off something this big with a portal, doing it during a full moon would make it easier—and a super blue blood moon would simplify matters even more. Not that what they're doing could ever be described as easy. It's impossible. Well, previously thought to be impossible."

"Was that what caused the fire?" I asked her. "Yanking something as big as a house from one world to the next? Was it like…I don't know, interstellar friction or something?"

"Size shouldn't matter. When larger objects are brought through a portal, they don't burst into flames."

Yasha grinned. "Size does not matter?"

Kitty patted his hand—his enormous hand. "The bigger the

object, the more power needed to bring it through, but friction doesn't enter into the equation. I have no idea why Rake's house burned. Adding people, especially terrified people, to the mix would merely increase the amount of power needed." She paused, brow creased in thought. "Though… Again using portals as an example, if a powerful mage is being forcibly taken through a portal, the more the mage uses their magic to resist, the more power and effort is needed to keep that portal open and stable. Rake, do you know if your mage fought back when he felt himself being taken? Or whether he attempted to shield himself?"

"Yes, to both."

"That could have been what disrupted the signal. A better way to describe it might be dissonance, the presence of two opposing powers, one pushing, one pulling, both attempting to override the other. It could've caused tension or even friction, if you will, to a level that when your house arrived here, it burst into flames. It's just a theory, but it might explain what happened."

"It's the only one we've got," Rake said. "It'll work until a better one comes along."

I had a thought. "It wasn't a full moon in New York when your house dropped in. Was it a full moon in Regor?"

"As a matter of fact, it was," Tam said.

"How about the other buildings taken here?" Kitty asked.

"We don't know," I told her. "Though Kenji might have worked up a spinning 3D model based on the dates he's gathered for the other disappearances. In fact, I can virtually guarantee it."

"The moon wouldn't necessarily need to be full," she

added. "The gravitational effects of the moon are just as strong during a new moon as they are when the moon is full."

I snorted. "He'd be thrilled to hear it. He'd get to make even more adjustments to his model. Now that we know how Marek is doing it, all we have to do is figure out how to make him stop. Permanently."

24

Thankfully, it wasn't Marek and his megamage cabal against the handful of occupants of an obscenely expensive Las Vegas party suite.

We had the brains and muscle of the entire SPI organization behind us. They were working on the problem.

So were we.

While we could have unlimited boots on the ground within hours, we couldn't simply kick in the doors to Marek's penthouse suite, take the generator and crystal, and fight our way out.

Why?

In a word—magic.

One of the local SPI agents was essentially a human magic detector. Ian had just gotten his report. He'd gone into the Phoenix wearing a black suit similar to the uniform worn by the hotel staff. He'd added a gold nametag and fake ID on a lanyard around his neck to add to his bona fides. He hadn't attempted to get into the penthouse or theater. All he'd needed to do was get close to both.

What he discovered was not good and only confirmed our suspicions.

Marek and the Silvanus brothers had turned the Phoenix's penthouse and theater into the Vegas hotel version of Fort Knox. The outer perimeter was wrapped in wards and patrolled by Khrynsani agents glamoured as human security. And that was the light stuff. From there, Marek and Isidor had really laid it on thick.

So, even if we could bust through all that, it'd involve a magical battle that'd make any lightshow Vegas could ever dream of pale in comparison.

"Sounds like we're not storming the castle," Ben muttered to me while Ian told us the local SPI agent's findings.

"Has Kenji been able to get hold of a list of who'll be in the audience, or even who's staying at the hotel?" I asked.

"He has not. He said he encountered a level of security on the Phoenix's computers that is far beyond normal for a hotel."

"Cyberwards," Rake said.

"That's how he described it. It doesn't change the parameters of the mission—disarm the terrorists, free the hostages. That magetech generator is just as dangerous as a bomb, and every person inside that hotel is a hostage. The cabal will use that generator and crystal to incite terror." Ian's expression hardened. "Dr. Cheban and her team cannot say with certainty that there will not be fatalities if the building is removed from Las Vegas."

"Because Tulis is a mage and could protect himself, and the people in the audience tonight aren't and can't?" I asked.

Ian nodded. "She believes that if humans were used in previous tests and survived, it doesn't mean that all of those in the audience tonight would do the same. Age and overall physical condition could mean the difference between life and death."

"So younger people would live, and older people could die."

"Not on our watch," Yasha growled.

"I'm with you, buddy," Ian told him. "We have several mundane options. Headquarters could call in a very plausible bomb threat before the theater opened its doors tonight, forcing Marek to cancel the show."

"Which wouldn't necessarily stop Marek from taking the hotel," Rake said, "but there wouldn't be anyone in the audience to see him do it, which would suck all of the fun out of it for him. I think he'd pull the plug at that point, unless those pulling his strings made him go through with it."

"We could also cut the power to the hotel," Ian said. "The hotel staff would be forced to evacuate everyone. While that would stop Marek tonight, he and his gang would merely choose another night, another building, different people. To take a smaller building with fewer people, all he'd need would be a ley line running beneath it or nearby, and a normal full or even a new moon. Would that be correct, Kitty?"

"Based on what we know now, yes, I would say that's correct."

"There are entirely too many strategic sites that would be

vulnerable to such an attack. For example, Washington, DC, has ley lines that not only flow through the city, they intersect, thus magnifying their power. Ms. Sagadraco has decided, and I agree, that we must finish this tonight."

"So we *are* storming the castle?" Ben asked.

I saw the twinkle in my partner's eyes and grinned. "I'm guessing more along the lines of a stealthy infiltration."

Ian smiled and brushed the tip of his nose with his index finger.

As if our situation and surroundings weren't surreal enough, now Ian and Rake weren't just working together, they were working together well. A coconspirator level of well. Tam and Gethen were right in there with them. The four of them were thick as thieves. Which, when you thought about it, was exactly what we were. The magetech generator and Nidaar crystal didn't belong to us, but they shouldn't belong to anyone, most of all Marek Reigory.

Ben Sadler had gone from being excited about storming the castle, to freaking out about his role in said incursion.

Shut down the crystal.

At least, that's how Ben understood Tam's intentions.

"Two days ago, I didn't even know these things existed, and now you want me to stop...*that* from vanishing?" Ben waved his hand at the hotel floorplan projected on the giant screen in the media room. Rake had scored the floorplan through his contacts and had hooked up his laptop to the screen. For tonight's plan to work, it was critical that we all memorize the hotel's layout.

"With a gem mage of your strength, the size of the crystal doesn't matter." Tam had been trying to sell that line to Ben since yesterday. It'd been an easier sell out in the desert when the lives of thousands hadn't been hanging in the balance. "As our fleet neared the coast of Aquas, the Khrynsani activated the Heart of Nidaar, causing what you call a tsunami to rise behind our ships. Agata Azul, using only the crystal in her pendant, pushed back against the mage controlling the Heart of Nidaar, calmed the wave, and saved our fleet and hundreds of lives. All you need to do tonight is disrupt the connection between the generator and the crystal."

"Small potatoes," I chimed in.

Ben shot me a look.

"Just you in the same room with them while wearing that ring might be enough to do it." Tam paused, a very slow smile curled his lips, the confident smile of a man who'd just discovered he was holding all the right cards. "In fact, with our plan, all you may need to do is deactivate the two small crystals in Marek's cuffs."

Rake nodded in approval. "If he's cornered, his first impulse will be to use those cuffs and disappear."

"And if he's near that generator," Ian said, "he'd grab it and teleport out. We won't have any idea where he's gone, and he'll be able to do this again somewhere else. Now that the cabal is finished testing, we won't get any warning next time. We have to do this now, and we have to do it right."

Ben blew out his breath. "In other words, 'Man up, Ben.'"

"I didn't say that."

"You didn't have to." He looked to Tam. "I just don't want to screw this up."

"You won't."

Ben sighed in resignation. "Okay then."

Too bad Caera Filarion wasn't here. She was a member of SPI's magical skills assessment team, and had been Ben's introduction to the supernatural side. They'd hit it off. Big time. Caera would've been able to have peeled Ben and his nerves off the ceiling with a little bedroom fun time. It'd worked wonders for me.

"I would be glad to rip arms off of mage," Yasha offered. "We get cuffs and stop cabal."

"You're a little furry for public consumption, buddy," Ian told him.

Yasha held up an amulet. "I have charge left in glamour. Kitty is going. I will not stay here."

I glanced over at my friend. "You're going?"

"I'm the getaway driver." She unfolded her legs where she'd been curled up in a corner chair. "In fact, I need to get to work. I'll be setting up a portal here, and once we get what we came for over at the Phoenix, I'll rip a portal there to escape back here with the crystal and generator. Tear it there, come out here."

Kitty could open a portal to anywhere in midair—no fancy frame, no runes, no crystals, just Kitty power.

I raised my empty coffee mug. I'd finally deemed myself properly caffeinated. "Tear Marek and the Silvanus brothers a new one. I like it."

25

"Are pets allowed?" I whispered to Rake.

Werewolves had great hearing, too. Right now, Yasha and Kitty were relaxing in the hot tub out on the terrace to try to take the edge off Yasha's werewolf urges. The tub was surrounded by what the hotel's website called the Zen Garden. Since it was completely private, Yasha was letting his hair down, so to speak, for as long as he could before he had to bottle it up with a glamour for tonight. He was pretty much still in his human form, but jeez, was he furry.

Rake kept his voice down, too. "In this suite, anything's allowed if you're willing to pay to repair the aftermath. Within reason."

Kitty had just skimmed a handful of hair the length of Christmas tinsel off the top of the water.

"Is werewolf fur in the hot tub jets within reason?"

"Completely."

"We're gonna need more towels."

"They're on their way up."

"He *is* like a sasquatch," Ben said in awe.

Ian didn't even look up from his phone's screen. "Sasquatches have less hair."

The plan was set, pieces were still being put into place, but we were all taking advantage of the time we had to relax before we needed to leave for the Phoenix.

The show was sold out, but Cassandra du Vien had a box at the theater for tonight's show. Marek had offered it to her personally. That was brazen as hell. A fake vampire offering the vampire mistress of a city and her court tickets to a show where the hotel would disappear and probably kill them all. Or re-kill. I really didn't know how that'd work with vampires. Though I could imagine how it'd gone when Alain Moreau had called Cassandra du Vien and told her what Marek's plan was. He had asked her to give us her tickets and stay away from the Phoenix. Surprisingly, she had agreed—at least for her court. We could have their tickets, but she was keeping hers. Marek might be suspicious if she didn't show. He didn't know her court, so the eight of us glamoured and there with her wouldn't arouse any suspicion. Besides, if there was anything left of Marek when the dust settled, she'd told Mr. Moreau, she wanted a piece of him.

I wouldn't be meeting Cassandra du Vien until she arrived at eight o'clock tonight to go with us over to the Phoenix, but I liked her already.

☙

Human form or not, after Yasha finished his soak with Kitty, he did a respectable imitation of a big red dog shaking off water. And rather than kill every hairdryer in the suite trying to dry himself, Yasha went with some sunbathing. I had to admit, the Las Vegas midday sun and desert wind did wonders for drying a werewolf without leaving him looking like a giant Pomeranian. Well, that and a little judicious grooming from Kitty. And board shorts, definitely board shorts, for which we were all grateful.

"I was thinking," Yasha said to Tam. "Are magic cuffs a goblin thing? If so, why have they not shared with SPI?" He gave Rake a slightly accusing, increasingly yellow-eyed glance.

Yasha and Kitty didn't know Tam from Adam's house cat, having only met him when they showed up at our suite door. Yet Yasha instinctively knew that if Marek's cuffs were a goblin technology, it had to be Rake's fault that SPI didn't have any for our own use. What can I say? He and Ian were brothers from other mothers.

While Tam told them the background of the cuffs and the Sythsaurians who made them, Yasha excused himself to quickly pad off to the kitchen to get more of the steak tartare Rake had had sent up from the restaurant.

"Reptilian invaders from outer space?" Kitty asked, when Tam had finished. "I guess the trope had to have to come from somewhere."

"Bi-pedal alien lizard invaders sounds better than what we have on our hands right now," I said.

"It sounds like a movie I saw once on *Mystery Science Theater 3000,*" Ian said.

"A *bad* movie," Rake muttered.

"But in a good way," I said. "I like *MST*."

"They're all bad movies on *MST*." My partner glanced around. Yasha hadn't come back yet. "Don't tell Yasha I said that. He thinks those movies are the golden age of film."

"I heard that," Yasha called from the kitchen.

I thought for a moment. "Which brings up something I've wondered about, especially since coming to work at SPI. Why do we keep trying to contact extraterrestrials? Hasn't it occurred to anyone that there are homicidal maniacs in space the same as there are here? What are the chances that if we do make contact, we'll attract the attention of cute, little ET aliens instead of a race of lizards who think all we're good for is food?"

Ian leaned back and stretched his legs out in front of him. "Hopefully we're too far down on the evolutionary scale to be worth noticing."

"Or taste bad," Yasha added, padding back from the kitchen. Getting words around his increasingly werewolfy dental work was a challenge. "Space travel must be like road trip. You do not stop at places with bad food. Little green men have been here before. Have not been back." The Russian werewolf shrugged. "Earth must be greasy truck stop of universe."

"We can only hope, buddy," Ian said. "We can only hope."

We knew the magetech generator would be the centerpiece for the show's finale, but we really didn't know what it'd look like.

Now we did.

The hotel's PR people had released a special ad for tonight's show. It was on the hotel's website, the marquee in front of the hotel, and on digital billboards up and down the Strip.

We assumed the representation of the magetech generator was accurate.

Again, Marek Reigory was being brazen as hell.

"Now he's thumbing his nose at God," I said. "That's not gonna go over well."

The magetech generator had been designed to look like the Ark of the Covenant—or at least the version that'd been in *Raiders of the Lost Ark.*

"I'm assuming the crystals are inside," I said.

"He must not have seen the movie," Ben said in disbelief. "Opening that thing was not a good idea, let alone messing around with the insides."

I shrugged. "When you think about it, the design's well chosen. From what Tam said, that's the kind of power we're talking about here."

And our job was to open it and take out the crunchy crystal filling.

You could buy pretty much anything you wanted in Las Vegas—if you had the money.

Rake did.

Though even his credit card had to be smoking after this.

Within the next two hours, formalwear started arriving.

We'd left New York thinking we'd be making a quick trip

to the Nevada desert to have a look around. We'd all been wearing clothes for doing that. Outdoorsy, hiking-type stuff. Technically, we were still in the desert, but we were way underdressed for tonight's activity.

I had no idea how he'd done it, but Rake had taken care of everyone's wardrobe needs. When you waved whatever kind of plastic billionaires carried, you got service and you got it fast.

I had to admit, we looked as hot as Rake's credit card.

Rake and Tam's tuxes hadn't been delivered to the suite. They'd just shown up, which told me there was something to Rake's duffel bag being of the Mary Poppins variety. I recognized the tux Rake was wearing from a party we'd attended last month, and the one Tam wore from the party before that. It came in handy that they were the same height, build, and size.

Ian and Ben weren't Rake's size, so he'd had to order out for their formalwear.

My sweetie had flawless taste, so my partner and our team gem mage looked like a million bucks. I made Ben stand still for a quick photo with my phone to send to Caera when this was all over. I knew she'd want to see her man all spiffied up.

Kitty and I were close to the same size, and Rake had done an excellent job guessing for her. This wouldn't be the first time Rake had bought evening wear for me, and I'll admit to some trepidation unzipping the garment bag.

Wow, that was a surprise.

A black, one-shoulder jumpsuit—with no parts cut out, see-through, or simply missing.

The bodice was snug, and the legs were loose and flowy,

but not so flowy that it'd trip me. I could look good *and* move fast. Usually, those two did not go together. There was even a built-in bra to ensure that the girls wouldn't try to, shall we say, venture forth on their own even if I had to run for my life, which I thought was increasingly likely.

In another surprise, Rake had included panties, though they were little more than strategically placed silk and scraps of lace, also in black.

I smiled. You couldn't beat the classics.

I'd feel like a sexy ninja. Now if I could just learn to fight like one.

Kitty was in a jumpsuit as well, but hers was capri length with a cute little detachable skirt over it. Rake had even gotten flats for both of us. I would've preferred something along the line of running shoes, but for Rake to go from buying me four-inch heels to no heels…? That was a huge step in the right choosing-clothes-for-me direction.

Yasha got a gander at Kitty's silk-wrapped legs through a slit in the skirt, and he whistled. A wolf whistle, of course.

Rake even managed to find a tux for Yasha.

Only in Las Vegas were there tuxes that were held together with snaps.

Apparently, there was a male stripper somewhere in this town as big as Yasha. I did not want to go to the bachelorette party where he'd be performing. Some girls might be into that, but the sight of that much man would send me screaming into the night, and not in a good way.

I had to admit that a stripper tux was the perfect choice for a werewolf during a supermoon. If Yasha had to go wolf, he wouldn't tear his tux to shreds and be standing around naked afterward. Since Kitty would be responsible for our getaway portal, Yasha was her self-appointed bodyguard for the evening. Kitty volunteered to keep up with any of Yasha's discarded clothes.

I had a sneaking suspicion that *The Hangover* was going to pale in comparison to our upcoming evening.

We didn't have a tiger in our suite; we had a werewolf.

26

Ben's instincts were right on target, and so were the military satellites Kenji had hijacked.

They'd found the missing buildings.

They were in a canyon about a hundred and fifty miles east of Shiloh City. That bit of news gave Ben a much-needed shot of confidence.

In the immediate area was an old silver mine.

"We've gotten heat signatures from inside the mine," Kenji was telling us from the media room's screen. "A lot of them, and they're moving around." He gave us a big, happy, but tired grin. "That mine hasn't been operational since the 1890s. It has to be their base. In a couple of hours, we'll know for sure. We're sending in commandos and battlemages to take it." Kenji looked off to the side as someone spoke to him.

"Oops, I jumped the gun. Mr. Moreau will be briefing you on that in a few minutes."

"How close are the buildings to the mine?" Ian asked.

Kenji glanced down at his keyboard. "I can let you see for yourself. Here's the enhanced satellite image." Kenji's face was replaced by an incredibly detailed photo.

"Dang, those military satellites *are* good," I said. "Marek and Friends made their own ghost town."

"Some of our tax dollars do good work," Kenji replied. "As you can see up in the far-left corner, one of the buildings landed on its side and kind of collapsed in on itself. From the information we've managed to gather, that was the first building taken. Their aim got better after that. In the center of the image, you can see where the last few were lined up like they were on a street. Lucky for us, the skies were clear and sunny today, so we got really good detail." He zoomed in on the line of buildings to show us. "I imagine if you were on the ground there, it'd look like that scene from *Close Encounters of the Third Kind* where the missing ship showed up in the middle of the desert. Well, except buildings aren't as out of place in a desert as a ship, but you get what I'm saying."

"Other than the heat signatures in the mines, have you detected any signs of life inside the buildings?" Ian asked.

Kenji came back on the monitor. "None. That doesn't mean there weren't any survivors. They could be in the mines, or the buildings taken were vacant. Another indicator this is their base is that the ley line that runs down the Vegas Strip leads right to the mine's front door." He glanced away again. "Oh, okay. Claire wants to talk to you." Kenji rolled his chair to the side, and Dr. Cheban rolled hers into the frame.

"We've determined there would need to be a second generator and crystal in the mine to function as a beacon," she told us. "It would be larger than the one Marek is using in his show. There's a shaft that runs from the deepest part of the mine straight up to the surface. We think that's where they have it. When the mine was operational, there would've been a lift to bring miners and supplies into the mine and back to the surface. Of course, the cabal wouldn't be using the original lift. This way the beacon can be raised when needed and lowered to keep it from being detected. There're also tracks for carts to bring silver ore to the lift. The cabal is probably using these to take the generator deeper into the mine when it's not in use."

I grinned and nudged Ben. "Except they couldn't hide it from our Level Ten master gem mage here."

Ben smiled and blushed.

"Marek's 'illusion' won't work if the device in the mine is incapacitated," Claire continued. "Kenji and I will be going with the team to the mine. Ian will be our contact with your team. We'll keep you apprised of events there as they happen."

"Sounds good," I told them. "Maybe after all this is over, you two can come down here. With all that math genius, I'll bet you two would make a killin' in the casinos."

Kenji leaned over into the screen, his head next to Claire's. They exchanged guilty looks. "Yeah…about that. We're kind of banned from the bigger casinos," he confessed.

Claire laughed. "We won too much on our last trip."

I blinked. "*Last* trip? *We?*"

They exchanged another look, this one with absolutely no guilt whatsoever.

"Oh honey," I told Kenji. "We are *so* gonna talk when I get back."

He was all innocence. "Whatever do you mean?"

Claire smiled and waved as she moved out of the frame, followed by Kenji. "Mr. Moreau wants to talk to you," he said on his way out.

When Alain Moreau took a seat in front of the camera, he wasn't smiling.

Uh-oh.

"Bad news, sir?" Ian asked.

"More like a confirmation of suspicions, Agent Byrne. We already had proof linking Marek Reigory to the other mages on our most-watched and wanted lists, but we now know who is in charge of them all."

Moreau clicked a few keys and on the screen was a photo featuring Marek and two mages from the list, Griselda Ingeborg and Gerald Blackburn. But it was the two others in the center of the photo that rolled the breakfast in my stomach.

If "impending doom" had human form, it would be Viktor Kain and Tiamat.

Though human wasn't the real form of either one of them. They were dragons. Thousands-of-years-old dragons.

"This is from a reception after Marek's performance in Moscow late last year," Moreau was saying. "Tiamat and Viktor were his guests of honor. Griselda and Gerald were seated in the royal box with them."

I was definitely feeling queasy. "Is there ginger ale in any of the fridges?" I heard myself ask anyone with working legs. Mine had gone kind of wobbly. "I could really use some."

Rake went to the bar fridge in the back of the room, and

seconds later I heard the blessed pop fizz. It wouldn't calm my nerves, but maybe it'd placate my stomach.

"They all looked nice and cozy," Ian said. "And guilty as hell."

I took a swig of ginger ale. "Can you say conspiracy?"

"Can you say cabal?"

Yep, with Viktor and Tiamat involved, we definitely had one of those. I took another swig, bigger this time.

Tiamat, aka the Babylonian dragon goddess of chaos, aka Vivienne Sagadraco's sister. According to the boss, Tia had always resented having to hide what she was. The problem with having a civilization worship you as a goddess was that you started believing your own PR. Tia wanted the human race to know they weren't the top of the food chain. She had two uses for humans: slaves and food. Sounded like the Sythsaurians. Oh, we did *not* need for those two to meet. Tia wanted to destroy what her sister had done through SPI—keep the supernatural world secret from humans, thus protecting humans and supernaturals alike.

In my first big case at SPI, Tia had gotten her hands on a device that rendered its wearer unseen and unheard. She also imported a pair of breeding grendels and equipped them with the devices with the intent of turning them and their hungry brood loose in Times Square on New Years' Eve. After that, armed with the devices, her ghoul and demon allies would be capable of appearing and vanishing at will. Humans would live in constant fear, banding together, never sure when or where the next attack would come from. Life on Earth would become a living nightmare.

Tia had gotten her claws on an even more impressive gadget this time.

Riding with Tia on the crazy train was Viktor Kain. He was a Russian dragon, oligarch, head of an international crime syndicate, and Ms. Sagadraco's personal nemesis. He blamed her for the death of his mate Katarina during WWII. British fighters flown by SPI agents had shot her down after she'd destroyed SPI's London headquarters during the Blitz, killing hundreds of agents and their families who'd taken shelter in its underground buildings. Katarina had allied herself with the Nazis. They'd promised her part of England to be her hunting territory if she helped them destroy London.

I'd been briefly connected to the mind of Viktor Kain while in contact with a nexus of ley lines and the cursed diamonds known as the Dragon Eggs. We didn't have proof that it had anything to do with him, but we couldn't discount it, either. It was bad enough that some of the most powerful mages on Earth were working together against us, but to find their actions were being directed by Viktor Kain and Tiamat? Bad just turned into the worst-case scenario, and gave a whole new and unpleasant meaning to "power couple."

"Are Tiamat and Viktor in Las Vegas?" I asked.

"They have not been seen," Moreau replied.

We knew what that meant.

Those two had been alive for thousands of years. They wouldn't be seen unless or until they wanted us to see them.

I suddenly wished one of my mysteriously acquired skills was the ability to sprout eyes in the back of my head.

"Marek's show begins at nine o'clock. The moon reaches its peak at ten. That will be when he makes his move. We will be in position to strike at eight." Moreau smiled, more of a baring of fangs. "Do not be surprised if the show is suddenly canceled."

Ian laughed, short and harsh. "I assure you, sir, we'll get over it."

"But if Marek does cancel, that doesn't change your mission. Secure those crystals at all costs."

～ 27

Ian and Mr. Moreau talked for a little longer, as Ian gave him the final status of our plans. And yes, we had more than one. Failure was not an option. Success would depend on being able to adapt to changing circumstances. With Tiamat and Viktor running the show, we had no doubt many surprises would be pulled out of multiple hats.

And none of them would involve cute, fluffy bunnies.

"You wouldn't happen to have your spear, would you, Ian?" Rake asked after Mr. Moreau had signed off.

"I never leave home without it."

A single glow flared from beneath the collar of Ian's tux jacket. It was listening.

"Good. I have a feeling we will have need of it before this night is through."

Cassandra du Vien arrived just after sundown.

The mistress of the Las Vegas vampires was not in any way what I expected.

That made her even more awesome.

I expected pale and slinky, rather like Morticia Addams in black sequins.

Cassi du Vien—and yes, she insisted that we call her Cassi—was originally from New Orleans by way of Haiti. She was curvy and confident, bold and bodacious. Anyone who saw us walk into the Phoenix with her would totally believe we were her entourage; that is, if they even noticed us at all. She was wearing a form-fitting purple silk gown like the vampire queen she was. In her heels, she was nearly as tall as Rake and Tam.

She'd brought four guards with her. We didn't take it personally. Heck, we welcomed the help. Alain Moreau had called and told her that a goblin masquerading as a vampire was going to perpetrate one of the worst acts of terrorism in history while in her city. Thousands would disappear and possibly die, and they would do so in a way unexplainable to human technology.

It would set off a worldwide panic.

And depending on what Marek or his cabal cohorts did next, if they made it known it was alien technology combined with magic, every supernatural on Earth would have a price on their heads. We didn't know what their ultimate goal was, but we knew it would have worldwide implications, and SPI would be in the crosshairs of both sides.

Ian took care of the introductions, and Madame du Vien—excuse me, Cassi—couldn't have been more pleased with her company this evening.

"It's a shame you gentlemen have to glamour," she said,

taking in the scenery. "But, from what Alain told me, it's necessary, and the results will be more than worth it." She frowned, and I could see the sass building. "He's posing as a vampire, plucking that hotel and everyone in it right off the Strip, including me and my court, and then dropping the blame on my own people? I don't think so."

"Can we depend on your discretion this evening?" Rake asked diplomatically.

"Oh absolutely," she all but purred. Her large, dark eyes twinkled. "A spider doesn't wrap up her prey until he's good and tangled in her web. Alain told me what you have cooking for Monsieur Keram Rei, and you have my blessing. Now *that* will be a show I'll want to see."

"It's critical that we succeed tonight," Ian said. "If we don't stop this now, the next target could be a strategic political or military target like the UN or Pentagon."

Cassi gave my partner a flat look. "A hotel in my city isn't important?"

"It wasn't my intent to imply that, ma'am."

"There are more of my people within the city limits of Las Vegas than any other city in the world. They are like my children. I *will* protect them. For me, there is no target more strategic. Such an act committed here will bring attention to my people that they may not survive. All vampires would become suspect, both in the supernatural and mundane worlds. We would be hunted." She paused meaningfully. "And if we are hunted, we *will* fight back."

"Nobody wants that," I told her.

"No, they do not."

The deep red moon rising over the Las Vegas strip could have been breathtakingly beautiful, if it hadn't been for the act of evil it would soon be used to power.

Cassi and her guards took her limo to the Phoenix, with our limo right behind.

Even though I'd never been inside the hotel before, I was more than familiar with its layout. We'd studied the floorplans and photos of every section of the hotel. Thankfully, it wasn't that large, at least not as Vegas hotels went.

As soon as we'd passed the front desk, we were in the casino.

"They want to get you coming and going, don't they?" I remarked.

"To get anywhere in a Vegas hotel, you have to go through the casino," Ian told me.

"You've been to Vegas before?"

My partner's lips twitched in the slightest of smiles. "A time or two."

"Have *you* been banned from any casinos?"

"Not any *casinos*."

I grinned. "Oh really? We need to talk, too."

"You can ask, but I'll never tell. In case you haven't heard, what happens in Vegas stays in Vegas."

I turned to our furriest team member. "Yasha? Do you know anything about this?"

The werewolf stayed silent *and* made a cross-his-heart motion.

Now I *had* to know.

We'd already decided to break up into small groups once we arrived. We were all glamoured and needed to look around to see who else was there and gather any intelligence we could before the theater opened for seating.

Tam and Ben would remain with Cassi and her guards. Tam would guide Ben through a subtle search of the hotel for Marek's crystals and any hotel guests/cabal members wearing teleportation cuffs.

Kitty had conjured a portal in our suite and was prepared to tear an escape portal here. Once we had the crystals, we were gonna need to get the heck out of Dodge fast. Yasha was Kitty's guard, and Ian was in direct contact with Mr. Moreau, who was directing the impending commando and battlemage strike on the cabal's base.

Rake was with me while I looked for the glamoured among the glamorous. He was holding my hand to keep Marek or any other cabal member who might be here from sensing me. Gethen was Rake's perma-shadow.

We were all connected by nearly invisible earpiece comms. By being in small groups, we could use our comms to stay in touch with the rest of the team and not look like we were wandering around talking to ourselves.

Rake and I were doing what a lot of couples were doing, strolling around the hotel and seeing who was there to see. With everyone people-watching, my interest in others didn't stand out in the least. I saw quite a few famous people, and some merely famous for being infamous. Plenty of them were wearing designer evening wear and jewels, but no one was wearing a glamour.

We'd determined that we couldn't do anything to delay the show. That would just scare Marek into taking the generator and teleporting out. We actually needed him on stage with the thing. Which brought up a couple of questions. If our commandos succeeded in taking the cabal's base and Claire and Kenji disabled the beacon, Marek's generator and crystal wouldn't work, according to Claire. But would he still be able to teleport out of here? Did he need the beacon to get to the cabal's base? Or could he teleport to any location?

I was about to key my comms and ask Ian, when I saw Ben and Tam stop. I didn't think it was obvious to anyone else, but I could tell that Ben had spotted someone.

"Ben's got one," I whispered to Rake. "Let's stroll past."

There were no windows in the casino. I could see how people would gamble longer if they had no sense of time.

I sensed her before I saw her.

A mage of the darkest variety.

Griselda Ingeborg was at the baccarat table. Her white beaded gown was slit up to there and had a neckline that nearly plunged down far enough to meet it. Her blond hair was piled high and sparkled here and there with jeweled pins. She wore diamonds. Lots of diamonds. The men in the immediate vicinity were captivated by the ones that fell between her ample breasts.

That was what everyone saw. My seer vision saw a black haze that shifted with her every movement, like fog. It was the aura of a mage who regularly engaged in the blackest of magic, so much so that it left a permanent imprint on her.

Then I saw what Ben had seen. It may not have been the most intriguing in terms of bodily placement, but it was what we were looking for. Griselda was wearing a Sythsaurian cuff. Naturally, it was encrusted with diamonds, so many that the green crystal in the center was barely noticeable.

Rake's lips twitched at the corners. "Tam's going in for a little reconnaissance."

"Poor guy," I muttered. "Having to take one for the team."

"A giving man, my cousin. Always thinking of others."

Tam was slicing through the crowd with the ease of a wolf carving a path through a flock of sheep, his primal instinct focused on one blond sheep. People got out of his way. Tam had some seriously potent come-hither, and that he was wearing his hair loose like a sheet of midnight silk only intensified it. Heads turned, breaths quickened, and a couple of drinks were dropped. Griselda looked up and I swear I saw her pupils dilate from where we were.

Rake had done it to me before. I knew how my body had reacted. If Griselda was female and breathing, she was on the receiving end of much the same effect.

As the crowd closed back around them, my attention went to Yasha. How could it not? I could see through his glamour, and under it, Yasha had gone full-on werewolf. He and Kitty were within smelling distance of one of the restaurants, and I knew it had to be all Yasha could do not to attack the biggest steaks I'd ever seen, being brought to the table closest to the restaurant doors. But he was holding it together. Kitty was the very picture of poise and composure at his side. Yasha started to growl and Kitty pinched one of his paw pads, turning the growl into a chastised yelp.

Portions in casino restaurants were enormous. I guess they wanted you fueled up to play for another twelve hours before you had to stop again to tank up.

A dark haze appeared at the edge of my vision by the elevators.

It was a well-dressed man. Tall and distinguished.

At least that was what his glamour told the world.

I saw something else.

The dark haze told me he was a black-magic practitioner. The out-of-focus features told me he was wearing an embedded glamour, a combination of a permanent glamour to disguise his real face, combined with a ward to make him instantly forgettable to all who saw him.

Rake started walking away, and since we were holding hands, he was taking me with him. "Let's grab a drink and watch Tam."

"Wait. I see something better. A guy who's had permanent work done."

Rake was careful not to look where I'd been looking. "Embedded glamour?"

"Uh-huh. He doesn't want his real face seen or even detected."

Since I couldn't get an ID from his face, I focused on his body. Not the pieces and parts, but how he carried himself. You couldn't disguise that, at least not easily. Great actors could pull it off. This guy was no actor. He probably could've if he'd needed to, but it would've been heavy-handed, obvious. He wasn't bothering to do that and the way he carried himself told me why.

Arrogance.

This was a game to him, a highly entertaining game. He was enjoying himself. It was all part of a larger scheme.

His larger scheme.

Then I knew.

I'd seen his silhouette twice, standing on the other side

of a portal. Tall, slender, supreme confidence twisted into malicious arrogance.

Later I'd seen him in person, after he stepped out of the best veil I'd ever seen. A veil that had seamlessly blended his entire body into a stalagmite.

High-elf arrogance personified.

Rake's nemesis.

I tightened my grip on Rake's hand before I said anything.

"Isidor Silvanus," I whispered.

Rake froze beside me, but to his credit, he didn't look. I knew he wanted to do more than look. He shifted, and I squeezed his hand. Hard.

"Focus," I told him. "He's not our mark tonight."

"The hell he isn't."

Isidor got on the elevator.

Rake growled. "He's getting away."

"No, he's not. He'll be back. If not tonight, some other time. Delayed gratification, darlin'. Embrace it."

I slowly felt the violence drain out, leaving him as calm and serene as a mountain lake.

I patted his hand. "The best way to ruin Isidor's life is to ruin Marek's night."

28

Ben spotted another member of the cabal.

Dietrich Wolf from Berlin.

A few minutes later, the doors to the theater were opened and a sea of people began flowing inside. Dietrich Wolf was arm in arm with Griselda Ingeborg. They were escorted to a staircase that led to the theater's boxes. Our group was led to the stairs on the opposite side of the lobby.

My arm was linked with Rake's. I leaned close to his ear. "Perfect. We'll be able to watch them." I glanced around and did a quick head count.

"Where're Tam and Ben?"

"Busy. They're checking something. They'll catch up with us later."

At the top of the stairs was a hallway with doors down

the left side leading to the boxes. A uniformed man bowed slightly as he opened the door to our box for Cassi.

We'd found photos of the theater, but none of them had done it justice.

It was a vision of classic Las Vegas extravagance. Chandeliers and gold. Everywhere and everything shades of gold. Oddly enough, it wasn't tacky. It was surprisingly elegant and tasteful. To pull that off was nothing short of a stunning interior decorating achievement.

When we sat, Rake kissed my hand and released it.

I suddenly felt naked, in a defenseless kind of way. "Are you sure that's safe?" I asked him.

He gazed into my eyes. "I wouldn't have let you go if you weren't safe." His brow creased in confusion. "You can't feel the wards?"

"I think my skin's too busy crawling to feel anything." I rubbed my hands briskly against my upper arms. "They've got the AC seriously cranked in here."

"That's not air conditioning; it's Marek's wards."

I stopped rubbing. "Oh. Then yes, I feel them. They're supremely icky—and cold."

"I couldn't agree more. However, that 'icky' is effectively hiding all of us from detection. Marek and his people laid them on thick. From what I can sense, the wards have seeped out to cover the entire hotel and the grounds. You're safe everywhere now."

I looked across the way to where Griselda and Dietrich were seated with people I didn't recognize, either from a personal encounter or our most-wanted list. My seer sight detected a faint haze over all of them. I wasn't sure if a black magic aura worked kind of like secondhand smoke and contaminated everyone nearby, or if they all were practitioners. I told Rake and Ian.

"Intriguing," was all Rake said.

"Apprentices?" I asked. "Here to witness an evil master plan in action?"

No response from Rake, but his eyes never left the box and its occupants as the lights dimmed.

Showtime.

Rake leaned over to Ian and they talked quietly for a few moments. I was sitting near the box's curtain, which conveniently allowed me to see everything I wanted to see, but at the same time I couldn't be seen by anyone in the Chock Full o' Evil box across the way.

As dramatic music swelled to fill the theater, Ian turned away from the sound and anyone watching, and raised his hand to his ear. A few seconds later, I saw his lips move in his favorite word of expressing extreme annoyance.

He leaned over to me. "Mac, Kitty's having problems with her comms."

Crap. Kitty's portal was our getaway. We had to be able to talk to her. Yasha didn't have any comms because his werewolf ears were too big. He and Kitty were at the poolside bar, which was outside the hotel itself, enclosed by trees and gardens and surrounded by a wall that wasn't attached to the hotel building. If the hotel was taken, they would be safe. The bar area was easily accessed from the theater. We thought it'd be the best place for Kitty to set up shop, and we all knew the quickest ways to get there from anywhere in the hotel.

Ian reached in his jacket pocket. "You've pointed everyone

out to us, so we're good for right now. I need you to take her a spare." He pressed the earpiece into my hand.

"You got it, partner." I put it in my purse and checked to make sure I had my ticket stub so I could get back into the theater. I held it up for Ian to see before I put it back. He gave me a thumbs-up.

I stood and miraculously managed to leave the box without tripping on anything or falling on anyone in the dark.

It didn't take me long to get to the pool area, but I went from a jog to a snail's pace when I got there. It was Saturday on a warm fall night in Vegas with a blood moon rising overhead. This place was jumping. It sounded like there was a live band here somewhere, but I couldn't see where they were.

I threaded my way through the crowd to where Kitty and Yasha were. They'd scored themselves a romantic little grotto, tucked away behind a hedge. Kitty had wisely ordered Yasha some of that raw beef sushi that I could never remember the name of. Judging from the empty plates on the table, he'd been packing it away.

A full werewolf was a happy werewolf.

When she saw me, Kitty's eyes got huge, and Yasha jumped to his feet with a growl.

"What's wrong?" she asked.

"Wrong? Nothing's wrong. I'm just here to give you Ian's spare comms."

Kitty looked confused. "Huh? There's nothing wrong with—"

"You didn't try to call him?" I asked, as the bottom fell out of my stomach.

"No."

I was furious. "He tricked me. He and Rake. They tricked me."

"What? Why?"

"They wanted me out of that theater."

I understood why they'd done it, but that didn't make me any less livid.

I turned to go back in.

Yasha's massive hand/paw wrapped around my upper arm. Literally. Engulfed the entire thing elbow to armpit. To any human who might have seen us, he looked like a really big, seriously intense guy.

"You have to stay here," I told him. "I don't. Your job is to protect Kitty and our way out. My job is in there." I bit back a growl of my own. "Even though some people don't agree."

"Mac, they had a reason," Kitty said. "They're trying to protect you."

"My job isn't to be protected. It's to point out what they can't see, and I can't do it from out here. I'll be back. We'll *all* be back."

When I got back to the theater doors, they were closed, and no one was at the box office windows. It was dark, like they'd turned off all the lights and gone home.

I tried the doors. They were locked.

Okay, *that* was a fire code violation.

I knocked. Nothing.

Harder. Still nothing.

I keyed my comms and called Ian.

Static.

Oh no. My heart skipped a couple of beats.

I called Rake.

Static.

Okay, girl. Calm down. Think.

What about Tam? Yes! He wasn't in the theater. At least I'd assumed he wasn't, from what Rake had said. I called him.

More static.

Screw comms. I got my phone out of my purse. No bars.

I cut loose with profanity's greatest hits. Too bad there wasn't anyone around to hear me. They'd have been impressed. Or appalled.

Fine. Thanks to the floorplans, I knew of other ways to get in, none of which were for the public, but I wasn't the public. Not anymore.

I was an agent of SPI. Protector of humans and the supernatural from the supernatural, and I had a job to do.

I was glamoured, but I wasn't a mage, so I had no way of making myself invisible.

That was a skill I could really use right now.

The doors that weren't locked were guarded or warded. *Heavily* guarded and warded. By Khrynsani mages. Rake had been right. When it came to his own security, Marek would go with his own people, and those people weren't about to let anyone in or out.

I silently recited the flip side to profanity's greatest hits.

"I don't care if you know where they're sitting," said a man's voice from around the corner.

I flattened myself behind a column, held my breath, and listened for all I was worth.

"And I care even less what that elf wants," he continued. "Don't move on them. Marek wants them taken with the others. There will be plenty of time for the elf to have his fun and games once we have—"

Another voice cut him off, but I couldn't make out a word he was saying.

"Because the hotel won't be there for them to find. The second base is operational as of—"

The other man cut him off. I still couldn't hear him.

"I answer to Mr. Kain, who, may I remind you, is paying your salary. Shall I tell him you're questioning his decisions?"

Silence.

"I thought as much. Tell the elf that as long as he's working for us, he will follow our orders. Understood? Good. Now get back to your station. I want to see the next part of the show before we leave."

I didn't so much as breathe until I heard them walk away and a door open and close seconds later.

And even then, I still wasn't breathing right.

Marek knew we were here. He wanted our team taken with the rest of the audience.

To another base. They had a second base.

Breathe, Mac. You're not going to do anyone any good if you pass out.

I gritted my teeth, breathing in and pushing it out, one after another, trying to calm myself.

No comms, no phone, no way to warn my friends.

But I might have one thing, and it was right around that corner.

A door.

A way into that theater.

29

I finally caught a break.

The door was unlocked. Better still, it led to the theater's backstage area, which was wonderfully dark.

I slipped inside.

What wasn't so wonderful was that half of those backstage were goblins with built-in night vision.

My seer vision didn't rely on light to tell me who was sharing any given space with me. Auras put off a slight gleam that was visible in all but pitch darkness. The only source of illumination I could detect came from the red glow of emergency lights. All it did for me was give the goblins around me a creepy red candy coating.

While I would've loved to have had some night vision goggles, that would've made me stand out more than I already did. I always tried to carry anything I might need in my purse. Rake had bought a little crossbody evening bag to go with my jumpsuit, and it only had room for the essentials. I should've carried my backpack.

Everyone backstage seemed to have a job, so I tried to act like I had one, too. The key to not being questioned was to act like you should be wherever it was that you were. I needed to be able to see what Marek was doing on stage, so I purposefully set off in that direction.

I was halfway there when a goblin woman stepped in front of me, blocking my path.

"Why aren't you in costume with the other girls?" she snapped.

"Uh…my Jeep's in the shop and I couldn't get an Uber?"

"That's no excuse. You only have fifteen minutes. Go!"

There weren't any dressing rooms on the side of the stage I'd come from, so I darted off in the direction I'd been going. The woman didn't yell at me for going the wrong way, so I assumed I was headed where I was supposed to go.

I spotted the seven "other girls" standing together near the left side of the stage and got a look at what they mostly weren't wearing.

It was essentially a bodysuit, except the suit part was sheer mesh with strategically placed golden sequins and feathers. From what I could tell, I didn't have enough curves to lift those sequins and feathers over my strategics, let alone cover 'em up. Then there were the heels. Dang. Little, strappy bits of gold and sparklies, with heels as high as my hand was long.

Uh-uh. No way.

I got a not-so-polite push from behind. "Hurry up!"

Well, if we were all gonna die anyway, I might as well have a side order of humiliation to go with it.

There was an extra costume in the dressing room, and it was my size. Apparently, one of the girls hadn't shown up and I'd been mistaken for her. All this would work out fine—*if* she didn't come walking in anytime soon.

I changed and gave myself a quick look in the mirror. All in all, not half bad. Just as long as I wasn't supposed to be a dancer, I might even escape humiliation.

"Fat lot of good sex did," I muttered. I was a nervous wreck again.

I got my one defensive item out of my purse and stuck it into my cleavage. It was amazing how this mesh could make even my girls stand up and say howdy.

I joined the others, staying in the shadows, but still earning more questioning looks than I wanted.

I gave them a little finger wave. "I'm the new girl. I think she got the flu…or something contagious."

The girl next to me—who had no worries about filling out her costume—took an obvious step back from me.

With her out of the way, I could see out into the theater. I was on the opposite side from our box, so I could see Ian, Rake, and Cassi. Gethen was just visible behind Rake. Still no Tam or Ben, at least not that I could see.

They were safe. For now.

I had no idea where the base had been moved to, and no way to warn Kenji, Claire, and the team who had to be there by now—or to warn my friends here who'd somehow been discovered and were sitting ducks.

I felt myself hyperventilating again. This was way beyond

terrifying. If Marek succeeded, this entire hotel and everyone inside would be here one moment and gone the next. Gone to where? Somewhere on our world? Another planet? Gone with possibly no hope of ever getting home again?

Two of the girls had turned and were watching something behind us. The others took a glance and arranged themselves into two lines.

I turned to see.

Oh. My. God.

Freight elevator doors had opened, and the Ark of the Covenant, aka the magetech generator, was being unloaded. It was perched atop a golden platform that must have had wheels mounted under it, given the ease with which it was being moved. It even had poles mounted to each side for carrying—or in our case, for pushing—just like in the movie.

It was being wheeled over to us—eight sequined and feathered showgirls lined up four to a side.

Not only did I not have a plan to stop Marek from killing us all, I was about to help bring him the means to do it.

When we got our music cue to process onto the stage with the generator, I had a few ideas, but none that were worthy of being called a plan. Either the crystal would kill me, or Marek would, but I had to stop him.

The generator hadn't been activated yet. I was no mage, but I think I would've known if the thing had been switched on. Marek would do that once it was on stage with him. I couldn't imagine activating a magical weapon of mass destruction not being part of the show.

I was the last of the four girls on the back side of the platform. It was the best possible place not to be noticed, and I didn't even need to ask to trade with one of the other girls. I was glad they'd assigned the girl with the smallest boobs to the back of the line. As an added bonus, no one saw that I'd kicked off my stripper heels and was walking on my tippy toes.

Marek was speaking, his voice ringing out over the audience. Apparently, the generator was supposed to be the Ark of the Covenant—or at least the Vegas magic show version. Marek was telling the audience the story of how when armies carried the Ark in front of it, they couldn't be defeated. It sounded like something Nidaar crystals could do.

I stopped listening to him. Think, Mac. You've got to stop this before he flips the switch on this thing.

Wait. Maybe it *is* that simple. Maybe all I need to do is—

A boom like a clap of thunder shook the stage beneath my feet.

It came from the main aisle of the theater.

Tamnais Nathrach, chief mage of the royal House of Mal'Salin, chancellor to the goblin king, and heir (albeit temporary) to the goblin crown, had appeared in the aisle in a brilliant flash of light and smoke. He had dropped his entire glamour, except for one part. He'd given his skin a vampire's preternatural paleness. He was garbed in the leather armor and tall boots he'd worn when he arrived on our world, only now he had his archmage robes on top, open down the front, flowing behind him, the robe and his long hair blowing in an honest-to-God wind.

The audience thought it was part of the show and roared its approval.

I bit my lip to keep myself from doing the same.

Tam's clear voice rang the crystal in the chandeliers. "Keram Rei! Only the mightiest mage may command the forces you have imprisoned in the Ark. I challenge you, here and now, before these most noble witnesses, to a trial of strength and cunning, to establish once and for all, who is the master…" His lips twisted in a wicked grin. "And who is still the student."

I couldn't fight back my own grin, and I didn't even try.

Way to hide in plain sight and be brazen as hell while you did it.

The audience was eating it up.

Tam strode toward the stage as ruby flames rolled down either side of the aisle, turning it into his own personal red carpet. At the same time, his hands began to glow with what I knew to be some seriously offensive magic.

Marek Reigory was a goblin mage pretending to be a vampire magician.

Two could play at that game.

Marek's face went even paler than he'd already glamoured it to be. It was with rage, not fear. I didn't know if he knew who Tam was, but he knew *what* he was, and that a goblin mage at or above his own level of power had just snatched away control of his show.

Since the generator was on a cart, I had no way of knowing how heavy it was. But that didn't matter. I had to make this work.

The poles attached to the generator were just for show, but they appeared to be attached well enough for what I needed to do.

Everyone's attention was on Marek and Tam. It was now or never.

I gripped the pole in both hands and pushed with everything I had.

The generator *and* cart flipped over, and the other girls screamed and ran, leaving yours truly to take the blame.

Okay, the cart and generator were lighter than I thought. Either that or my time in the SPI weight room was really paying off.

I played to the crowd with an apologetic grin and exaggerated shrug.

"You!" Marek roared.

I dove behind the generator. He wouldn't dare hurt that.

But he would come behind it after me.

I ran around to the other side, Marek chasing me. No doubt we looked ridiculous. I heard the audience laughing and clapping.

Marek stopped, his hands and arms suddenly extended in front of him toward the audience as if preparing to launch an attack.

No, no, no.

Marek's face was distorted with effort. He wasn't attacking, he was being attacked. It wasn't Tam. He had just reached the base of the stage. An unseen force had pulled Marek's hands out and away from him. His sleeves pulled back, exposing the cuffs on both wrists.

With a sharp snap, the cuffs unlatched and went flying over the audience's heads toward the back of the theater and to a lone figure standing there.

Ben. Wearing Rake's protective robe.

I didn't think the gem mage expected the cuffs to come shooting at him that fast. Ben didn't have his catcher's mitt, so he did the only thing he could do.

He ducked and the cuffs slammed into the wall behind him, shattering on impact.

The audience loved it. They hadn't expected comedy, but they were going along for the ride.

Tam launched himself up and onto the stage to the delighted gasps of the crowd.

Marek had no way to escape—unless he was willing to activate the generator and risk surviving the journey.

Everything went into slow motion for me.

Marek's expression hardened as he made his choice. I'd seen the same look on Rake's face when he'd decided to run into his burning house to save Tulis.

The lid had come off the generator, exposing a single crystal, oblong, almost football shaped.

I knew what I had to do.

Marek and I dove for it at the same time, but I was closer and not encumbered by tight leather.

I grabbed it, tucked it against my body, and ran like hell.

30

I wanted nothing more than to run through the theater toward where Rake and Ian were, but that would put me on a path through the audience. Marek wouldn't care how many defenseless humans he had to kill to get that crystal back.

My primal instincts must have already realized that because I was now running, ducking, and weaving in the direction of the door I'd used to get backstage. Ian and Rake would approve. In that direction were Kitty and Yasha—and the escape portal. I wasn't thinking of it for myself, but I had to get the crystal as far away from Marek and the cabal as quickly as I could.

A portal back to the relative safety of our warded suite fit the bill.

There was chaos backstage, but not nearly enough. The door I'd used to get in was now blocked by two goblins.

I was scared spitless and couldn't see diddly squat.

I changed direction, feeling like the Vegas version of Tweety Bird trying to get away from Sylvester and his friends. I could be captured and the crystal taken, and I had to at least clear every living and undead soul out of the hotel before that happened—and hopefully incapacitate the goblins chasing me.

I paused long enough to pull down on a fire alarm.

A banshee shriek filled the hotel, and I swear I felt my ears start to bleed.

Agonized goblin screams filled the backstage. Goblins had *really* sensitive ears. The hotel was owned by elves. They didn't care if their alarms hurt goblins. They'd probably planned it that way. I was gonna owe a serious sorry to Rake and Tam.

I'd heard a banshee before, and it'd been bad, but the Phoenix's fire alarms were like an entire flock of the things. A fire alarm's job was to clear everyone out because it was simply too painful to stay. Humans and supernaturals were stubborn, and if there was any way they could ignore orders they didn't want to follow, they'd do it.

This alarm didn't give you a choice. It was flee or have your head split open with sheer volume and pitch.

On my way in, I'd seen a ladder running up a wall leading to a catwalk.

I spat my favorite Goblin cuss word in realization. I needed two hands to climb a ladder. One of mine had a death grip on the crystal of death.

I desperately looked around for something, anything, any way out of here.

The flashing emergency lights showed me the way.

A small platform with a railing around it.

A lift. A one-person elevator.

I ran over, jumped in, and slammed my palm down on the button.

Please, please, please don't let anyone push a button and bring me right back down.

Over the alarms came a howl—familiar to me, no doubt bone-chilling to everyone else.

Yasha, an overprotective werewolf hopped-up on super-duper blood moon power.

Four goblins were running toward the lift, and Yasha jumped in front of them, dropping his glamour, and ripped off his stripper tux—starting with the pants—to the horrified screams of every being backstage with working eyes.

Yasha waved to me as I escaped, wearing nothing but fur and a smile.

Yep, my partners always had my back.

The lift arrived at its destination, and within seconds, I was running down the catwalk toward the stage and the auditorium beyond. We'd studied the theater's layout, and supposedly in this direction was access to a narrow hallway for light and sound maintenance that looked out over the auditorium and led to the control booth in the back. There had to be other ways that led back into the theater itself, but I couldn't for the life of me remember where they were, or if they even existed. I could get to the boxes on this side, I could meet up with my team if they were still there, or I could blend with the crowd that had to be stampeding to get away from the alarms. The gowns some of the ladies were wearing covered even less than my costume.

I reached the section where I could see down into the auditorium. It was complete chaos. I desperately looked around for a familiar face. I didn't see either Tam or Ben. Part of me wanted to find Ben. I couldn't throw a frisbee, but I could flatout throw a football. The crystal was much heavier than a football, but I still should be able to put a decent spiral on it. And even if it hit the floor, the thing was indestructible, which was really too bad. If it could be shattered, the only hotel it'd be able to translocate would be a roach motel.

"Here she is!"

The shouter, and the man who blocked my way, was an elf. A familiar elf. I'd seen him just before he had dived through a mirror to escape me and Kenji in the restaurant at the Regor Regency Hotel.

Phaeon Silvanus.

Inventor of the magetech generator. The cause of *all* of this.

I didn't think. I just reacted. Violently.

I may have been the one with the football, but I tackled Phaeon Silvanus. He wasn't a mage; he was just an elf, an elf who needed his ass kicked.

Rake would rather have Isidor, but I had Phaeon right here and right now.

We fell to the floor, rolling and wrestling. I knew some dirty moves, but there was no way I was letting go of that rock, so Phaeon got to use his moves first, flipping me onto my back and making me lose my grip on the crystal. Before I could get my knee up, the elf was on top of me. I got one hand on his throat, the other fumbled around in my cleavage for my purse-sized pepper spray and let him have it right in the eyes.

The scent of jasmine and honeysuckle filled the air.

Perfume, not pepper spray.

I cussed like castanets, and speed-pressed that bottle nozzle for all I was worth. Judging from Phaeon's reaction, even though it wasn't pepper spray, it still hurt like hell.

Never hit a man when he's down. Kick him. Hard.

Then shove him into a supply closet full of lightbulbs and lock it with a chair jammed under the doorknob.

I scooped up the crystal and kept running.

The only unlocked door I found leading out of the theater put me on the hotel's roof where the screech of the fire alarms had been replaced by the scream of the Las Vegas Fire Department's sirens.

Nothing about this was good. At least not for me. In horror movies, you didn't go into basements or attics—or onto roofs. It wasn't like I had a choice. Any other doors had been locked or blocked.

I ran to the edge and looked down. Whoa. I didn't have a problem *with* heights. I had a problem of falling *from* heights.

I was at the front of the hotel, and the only way down was into the neon flames of the marquee with the ill-fated phoenix. While I'd developed some nifty new skills, none of them involved flight or regeneration.

As far as Vegas hotels went, the Phoenix's ten stories made it downright tiny. But it could've been a hundred and ten, and my problem wouldn't have been any different. Falling from either height would kill me, the only difference being the consistency of the end result. There had to be another way down, and I'd find it.

The pool bar. Yes! Kitty and hopefully Ben would be there. I hadn't seen him since I'd gotten the crystal. Maybe he'd made it outside to our rendezvous point. They'd see me waving and jumping, and I could throw the crystal to Ben. He'd be able to catch it. Maybe.

Let's see, I was at the front of the hotel, that'd put the pool bar—

"I thought I might find you up here," Marek Reigory called out as he stepped from behind one of the big air-conditioning units.

I clutched my crystal football tighter. "I'll spike this thing into the parking lot."

"Go ahead. My people should be waiting there now to retrieve it." He came toward me. "And then I can help you have a horrible accident—just like one of your SPI predecessors. Falling from the Empire State Building was rather cliché, but you must work with what you're given."

We were both having to shout to be heard over the AC units and the sirens. I could tell it was sapping the fun right out of his Evil Villain Speech.

"You look a little singed around the edges," I told him. Actually, his hair looked shorter, and the ends were smoking. I took a whiff. That was definitely the smell of burnt hair *and* leather. Good job, Tam.

Marek gave me an elaborate shrug. "When you play with fire, you have to pay from time to time."

There were two ways for me to escape. One was unlikely, given that it involved me getting past a thwarted and homicidal goblin megamage. The other was taking a swan dive onto concrete, or whatever was ten stories down. It was time to find a third option and fast.

Marek was close enough now that we didn't have to yell. It was a relief for both of us.

"What now?" I asked.

"You give me the crystal, and then do me the very large favor of jumping to your death. I promise it will be less painful than what I will do to you."

I clutched the crystal to my chest with both hands. "No."

He leaned wearily against the backside of a neon flame. "Excuse me?"

"You heard me. No. I'm not doing one thing to make this easy for you. You want the crystal, come and get it. You want me dead, you'll have to do it yourself."

With a sigh, Marek pushed off from the neon flame. "Very well."

There was a dark blur, and Rake slammed into him from the side. Gethen was nowhere to be seen. Looked like Rake had ditched his babysitter.

"Run!" he shouted.

Rolling, punching, and kicking followed. And zapping, lots and lots of zapping. Rake had said that his and Marek's blood link protected each against some of the other's magic. That must have been why there was zapping and no vaporizing. Moments later, I smelled burning hair and leather again. All that rolling around must have fanned the flames.

Marek was not having a good night.

The couple of times they managed to get to their feet, punches were landing. Hard. At least Rake's were. Tam must've really rung Marek's bell.

I didn't try to help. Rake wouldn't want my help, nor did he look like he needed it. He was doing more than fine on his own.

Ian crossed the roof to where I was, staring the entire time at the rolling, hissing, snarling, and now seriously smoking mass of battling goblins.

"Damn."

I nodded slowly. "You said it, partner."

Without another word, Ian reached behind his head and drew out the nearly two-foot-long spearhead from under his jacket. It no longer glowed when Ian touched it, but I sensed a thrum coming from it. Maybe since the blade now knew Ian better, it didn't feel the need for extreme PDA, just a quiet acknowledgment of affection.

He saw me looking and shrugged. "Just in case." His lips twitched at the corners. "By the way, nice moves onstage earlier."

I nodded once. "Thanks."

The goblin fight had kicked into high gear. There was an explosion, and the two of them flew apart. Marek looked like a tom cat on the wrong end of a nasty alley fight. I think I even saw a nick on the pointed tip of his ear.

Then he stumbled to his feet and dove off the side of the hotel.

Ian and I ran over to see him land lightly, turn around and make a gun with his index finger and thumb, pointed right at me. Then he vanished; at least it looked that way to Ian.

I could see through his cloaking spell as he ran away, occasionally staggering.

Rake stumbled to my side, catching himself on the edge of the roof's wall. "Where is he?" He was battered, but his eyes were blazing for Round Two.

Marek had now gotten as far as the Bellagio and had gotten his wind back. His cloak solidified, and he vanished even to my seer sight.

I wrapped my arm around Rake's waist and gave him a squeeze. "Gone," I told him. "He's gone."

He'd be back. We both knew it, but I wasn't going to say it. Not now.

Rake plopped down to sit with his back against the wall. "I told you to run," he said too loudly.

"And I told you no."

"What?" he shouted.

Yeah, I definitely owed him an apology for pulling that fire alarm.

"We'll argue when we're not both deaf," I shouted back at him.

Rake looked me up and down with a wickedly sexy smile. "Nice costume."

～ 31

Marek Reigory had gotten away, for now. When Tam showed up, the other cabal members in the audience had activated their cuffs and vanished, leaving Marek to deal with the fallout by himself.

We were off the roof and back in the hotel, the banshees had stopped screeching, and the fire department had deemed it to be a false alarm. According to the police onsite, a fire alarm had been pulled in the backstage area, but oddly enough, none of Keram Rei's stage crew were around to be questioned.

Rake had seen Isidor Silvanus in the theater, and the elf mage had activated his cuff and abandoned ship at the first sign of trouble.

I grinned and linked one arm with Rake and the other with Ian. "Which reminds me. I have a present for both of you. At least I think I still do. Let's go see."

We found Yasha when we got downstairs, and it took me a few minutes after that to find a way to access the theater's lighting maintenance level. When we got there, I was delighted to see that the chair was still tucked under the closet's door knob. Kicking and shouting in elven and English was coming from inside.

I stood to one side of the door. "Ta-da!"

A mischievous grin flitted across Ian's mouth. "Is that who I think it is?"

Rake chuckled. "Why yes, I believe it is."

Ian removed the chair, and Rake flung open the door to reveal Phaeon Silvanus cowering inside.

Ian took a whiff. "What's that smell?"

Rake laughed outright. "Is that your—"

"Perfume. Yes. I confused it with my pepper spray, okay? I sprayed him in the eyes, so it still worked."

Yasha took a deep sniff of his own, and I swear, it sounded like his werewolf snout sucked all the air out of the closet. "Umm, smells pretty."

Phaeon's eyes went wide with terror as he plastered himself against the back wall.

Ian was grinning at me. "Nice catch, Mac."

Those of us who were human dropped our glamours to make getting around the hotel a little easier. Rake and Tam altered theirs and did the same for Yasha. Descriptions had been given to the police of a few of the more visible troublemakers, and we'd rather our contributions to this evening's excitement go unrewarded.

I hid in a ladies' room stall while Kitty snuck backstage to get my clothes and purse, since the police really wanted to question the showgirl who'd broken a very expensive stage prop, and then had run off with part of it. Ian made arrangements with the Vegas SPI office to "appropriate" the broken magetech generator and have it shipped to our New York lab. Tam and Ben showed up with the shattered remnants of Marek's cuffs. Once I was back in my little black jumpsuit, we returned to our suite at the Nobu Hotel via Kitty's portal, prisoner in tow.

Since Phaeon had no magic whatsoever, we just locked him in the suite's steam room (without the steam), and asked Yasha to stand guard until arrangements could be made to get him on a SPI jet back to headquarters and a more secure confinement. Mr. Moreau had come into town after their unsuccessful taking of the cabal's base. Well, the base taking was successful, just not the cabal capturing. They hadn't found any sign that the buildings brought there had been occupied. Apparently, the Regor Regency incident had been their "people test." Mr. Moreau and Ian questioned our prisoner with Rake and Tam listening in. Phaeon was less than cooperative until Ian threatened to let Yasha in the steam room with him to do all the sniffing he wanted.

Between that and knowing his brother had abandoned him, Phaeon started talking. In fact, Ian and Mr. Moreau couldn't shut him up.

Isidor had done all the negotiating with Marek and the cabal. Phaeon had done his part of the partnership from his lab. To get the crystals, Isidor had to trade four of the second-generation magetech generators to Sandrina Ghalfari and the

Khrynsani. As to the chest of smaller crystals she had given to Isidor, Phaeon claimed not to know anything about them. Tam made arrangements to get a message to his people in goblin intelligence back home about those four generators.

The attack on the Regor Regency had been Isidor and Phaeon's audition to get into the cabal as essentially their R&D department. When the Regency job had failed, the Phoenix was their last chance at redemption. Such a public attack was supposed to have been the cabal's coming-out party on this world's stage. We had rained all over their party.

Oh yeah, Marek, Isidor, and their cabal friends would all be back.

When the sun began to rise over the Las Vegas Strip, Yasha returned to his human form—his ravenous human form. Rake ordered vast quantities of food sent up. He told the hotel kitchen he was hosting breakfast for out-of-town clients. Many, many clients.

We were exhausted, but were too keyed up to sleep, which was good because Vivienne Sagadraco had just landed in Vegas and was on her way to our hotel for a full report.

"Unlimited power in the hands of the last people who should have it," Ms. Sagadraco said when we'd told her what had happened since we'd left New York. "Those already possessing vast power believe they and they alone can control any power regardless of its magnitude. They have all been wrong, dead wrong, and people have died because of their arrogance." She poured herself a second cup of tea. "I have been keeping very close watch over my sister and Viktor Kain.

When either one surfaced, I would know about it—especially if they were together. They have been cultivating influential allies in countries all over the world and are building a power base. It bodes ill if Tia has taken the Silvanus brothers under her wing. Though without Phaeon, the cabal's ability to develop weapons such as the magetech generator has been dealt a severe blow." Her eyes sparkled over the rim of her teacup. "Excellent work, Agent Fraser."

"Thank you, ma'am."

"Phaeon said there are two additional completed generators in his lab," Mr. Moreau told her. "He told us the location. We have a team going to retrieve them now—unless Isidor got to them first."

"Does he have any colleagues who are capable of replicating his work?"

"No, Madame. Isidor insisted that he work alone to ensure secrecy."

"I do love it when our adversaries do our work for us."

"They also still have that chest of Nidaar crystals Sandrina gave to Isidor," Rake added.

Ms. Sagadraco took a sip of her tea. "I have no doubt they're still capable of mischief."

I guess it took being a multi-millennia-old dragon to consider a cabal of evil mages bent on world domination as "capable of mischief."

"Why do they want to do the whole take-over-the-world thing?" I asked. "I mean, they're already rich and powerful. I've always thought world domination would be too much work and not worth the trouble."

"My sister and Viktor's need for self-glorification for

themselves, and subjugation for any they consider beneath them, overrides any inconvenience they may encounter in the meeting of those needs. They believe it is their rightful place and think humans incapable of ruling this world. They believe that humans will ultimately destroy this world, and they have been preparing to step in to prevent that."

She paused at the disconcerted looks she was getting.

"Seven of these cabal mages were in New York when Viktor Kain had the Dragon Eggs on display at the Metropolitan," she reminded us. "Had they succeeded in acquiring those diamonds they would have magnified their powers to near godlike. There would have been little we could have done to stop them. Such individuals would rise to the top of any new world order that would be established.

"SPI is a worldwide organization," she continued, "and I have alerted all of our national directors of the new danger we will be facing. Tiamat, Viktor, and their minions will be less able to operate without being discovered and hounded."

I wondered how Marek would take to being called a minion.

"If their larger plans are thwarted, they may content themselves with causing chaos by exposing elements of the supernatural world to humans. If they can't have control, they'll settle for chaos."

"Are we talking Salem witch trials, but on a frenzied, global scale?" I asked.

Ms. Sagadraco nodded. "Just so."

"When it comes down to it, we humans are panicky, primitive, basically stupid, herd animals," I admitted. "Spook a few, and before you know it, you've got a stampede on your hands. Some humans are open-minded and would think that supernatural beings living next door would be unspeakably cool. But most would reach for the modern equivalent of torches and pitchforks. If you're different from them, you need to go—one way or another. They don't want their narrow minds expanded."

"Knowing that supernaturals can disguise themselves would simply spread the killing to any humans they didn't like or trust," Ian said. "It would be the Salem witch trials or even the Inquisition on a global scale, except without any trial. They would go straight to execution. Blood would run in the streets, and a lot of that blood would be human, because supernaturals would fight back. They'd protect their families just as humans would. And when you have supernatural strength and sometimes even magic, you'll come out at the top of the food chain. It would be carnage."

Tam nodded. "Even a mage of average talent is faster than your human guns, both in shielding and retaliatory strikes. Mages of exceptional skill can obliterate a battlefield full of soldiers in a single strike."

The room went silent at that.

When I'd first started working at SPI, about two years ago, Ian had told me SPI believed a powerful supernatural entity was planning a major event, and that it'd take a seer to expose it. Three my predecessors had been killed to keep it from being discovered.

I didn't know if plucking a hotel off the Las Vegas Strip with everyone inside while TV cameras recorded it, and thousands of witnesses watched, qualified as *the* major event. If it wasn't, I didn't want to think about what their next target could be. But that was our job, to not only think about it, but stop it from happening.

As far as we could tell, we'd gotten through tonight without major exposure. Only in Vegas could two "vampire" mages duke it out, complete with fireballs and lightning coming from their fingertips, and the people in the audience would take to social media calling it the best show ever.

The public had been entertained this time, but how long would we be able to keep fact disguised as fiction?

32

Rake and I were having brunch in bed.

We had just finished the best bubble bath I'd ever had in the biggest tub I'd ever seen.

Ms. Sagadraco had given all of us the next few days off, and we'd decided to spend it right here. Rake was having Kylie and Caera flown in from New York, making Ian and Ben very happy. The girls would also be bringing clothes for the guys. Rake had made himself happy having more clothes bought for me. I was completely fine with not going shopping. I was part of the reason why malls were going out of business. I loved online shopping. Gethen was happy that Rake was staying put.

Cassi du Vien had been very impressed with Tam's performance last night, and when she found out he was a nightclub and casino owner on his home world, she'd insisted on showing him her town. Tam had a date tonight with the vampire queen of Las Vegas. When Mr. Moreau had found out, he did something rare—he laughed.

"Should we warn Tam?" I asked Rake.

"Oh, he knows. Don't worry, my cousin can handle Cassi du Vien."

Rake took a bite of scone, a spot of butter remaining on his upper lip. With a lascivious glance at me, the tip of his tongue darted out and smoothly licked the butter away.

I met his lick and raised him a seductively eaten, chocolate-covered strawberry.

Yasha's voice boomed from the living room. "We should rent beach house together. Go on vacation."

"If we all went to the beach together, there'd be a kraken offshore within the hour," Ian told him.

I snorted a laugh. "Glad to hear Ian's being the voice of reason."

"Is true." Yasha sounded crestfallen. "I know! We go to mountains."

"I've got two words for you, buddy: rabid yeti."

There was laughter, with Yasha's being the loudest, then our friends' voices lowered. Or maybe they'd adjourned to the terrace. Now that he was human again, and at least a little less hairy, Yasha wanted to get in the hot tub again. He'd found his happy place.

I nestled back on the pillows. I felt safe now, but I knew it wouldn't last. "I'll gladly take krakens and rabid yetis over what's gonna be coming at us."

"They've always been coming at us," Rake told me.

"That's why they're on Vivienne's most-watched list. Though after last night, I imagine she's had them all upgraded to the most-wanted list. Tia and Vik are in this for the long game. It may be years before they make their next move."

"Or next week."

"Unlikely, but possible."

"Their game is evil."

"Yes, it's evil. It's also part of a bigger game, and this is how the game is played."

"Then we need to do something about changin' the rules. We got lucky last night. Next time we might be findin' ourselves gettin' the short end of the stick."

The edge of smile appeared. "Your Southern is showing."

"Bite me."

He gave a low growl. "I'd love to." He did—and oh so much more.

I dragged myself reluctantly out of the deepest sleep I'd had in weeks.

Rake was watching me with his dark and wonderfully mysterious eyes.

"I haven't given you your birthday present yet," he said.

"Oh yeah. I completely forgot." I smiled. "Though what you just gave me certainly qualifies as a present."

"I haven't forgotten, but on your birthday, my house dropped out of the sky and burst into flames."

"Then you tried to incinerate yourself by running inside." I held up a hand to stop any protest. "You had a good reason."

"A very good reason." Rake snuggled closer. "Then that night in the desert, looking up at the stars. It was very romantic…"

"Until I sensed Marek."

"Yes, that was a mood killer. Then yesterday when we were here in bed… You had a lot on your mind and needed to focus. And last night, I almost lost you."

"But you didn't."

"I figure I need to give you this before anything else happens." He reached over to his duffel bag next to the bed and pulled out a small velvet box.

I froze. "Oh, my God. Are you—"

"Not yet. Not unless you want me to."

"I…I have no words."

"I have some. Makenna, you know I love you, and I would love to spend the rest of my life with you, but I know you're not quite there yet. I'm willing to wait, if that's what you want. I intend to inform your mother of my intentions when we're there next month."

My mouth moved a little, and I think some sounds came out, but none of them could remotely be called words.

"If you're gonna be doing that, don't leave out Grandma Fraser," I eventually managed. "If you do, she's likely to—"

"I can only imagine."

"And imagine is all you want to do, believe me."

Rake opened the box.

I blinked. "A locket?"

"Open it," he whispered.

I did.

My mouth fell open. "That's the biggest diamond I've

ever seen that's not cursed." I quickly looked up at him. "It's not cursed, is it?"

"If it is, I'm taking it back." He took the locket out of the box. "May I?"

I smiled and bit my bottom lip. "Yes."

Rake fastened the chain around my neck and it fell to right where I'd be able to see it every time I looked down. Rake's eyes were doing the same thing, though his attention was on the pale, freckled setting, not the stone.

"When you decide the time is right, let me know and I'll have it set in a ring. But until then, you can wear it in the locket." He grinned. "Or…" His fingers were warm on my chest. "You can remove the locket like this…" With a snap the locket came off to reveal the contents. "You can wear the diamond as a pendant for everyone to see. Private for you and to show any friends you want, or public for the world to see. Your choice. Your timing."

I took a shaky breath. "This is a surprise."

"And I know you don't like surprises."

"I like this one," I said softly.

"I have one more present for you, though you won't be able to see it until you get home. It'll be parked outside your building. Or across the street if it's street-cleaning day."

"The Jeep?!"

"Yes, the Jeep. And you won't need to worry about moving it. I have someone doing that for you."

I couldn't help it, I squealed.

"Is that for the diamond or the Jeep?"

"Uh…yes?"

"It's more for the Jeep, isn't it?"

"Well, sweetie, don't take this the wrong way, but I'm not a sparkly things kind of girl."

Rake kissed me and pulled me down on top of him. "I noticed."

"I don't care about your money."

"I noticed that, too."

"You don't mind?"

"It's one of the reasons I love you. You love me, not my money."

"I do love you, you know."

"I know." Then he made a show of pondering something.

I pulled back a little. "What is it? I know that look."

"While we're here… It'd almost be a waste not to."

"Not to what?"

His eyes started to sparkle. "Since you don't like going to a lot of trouble, and since we *are* in Las Vegas…"

"Yes?"

"Do you want to get married by Elvis?"

I gave him a playful smack. "Grandma Fraser would hunt you to the ends of the earth and beyond if you deprived her of a wedding."

"I cannot wait to meet this woman."

"Remember, you asked for it."

The End

⌒ ABOUT THE SERIES

Thanks for reading *The Phoenix Illusion*. I hope you enjoyed it! Reviews help other readers find books and I appreciate all reviews, whether positive or negative. Please take a moment and write a review for *The Phoenix Illusion*.

Suggested reading order for the SPI Files series:
The Grendel Affair
The Dragon Conspiracy
The Brimstone Deception
The Ghoul Vendetta
The Myth Manifestation
The Phoenix Illusion

I also have a story in the *Night Shift* anthology, containing *Lucky Charms*, a SPI Files novella.

You may also enjoy my Raine Benares series. For me, writing the SPI Files was a natural progression from my Raine Benares novels. From their covers, these books may look like traditional fantasy, but I wrote them with a modern urban fantasy tone—full of the type of action and humor found in the SPI Files. In short, if you like Mac, you'll love Raine. And if you love Ian and Rake, you'll go gaga over Mychael Eiliesor and Tam Nathrach. My Raine Benares novels are packed with adventure, intrigue, hot elves, and sexy goblins. There are sample chapters on my website at lisashearin.com.

Suggested reading order for the Raine Benares series:
Magic Lost, Trouble Found
Armed and Magical
The Trouble with Demons
Bewitched and Betrayed
Con and Conjure
All Spell Breaks Loose
Wild Card (a Raine Benares novella)
Wedding Bells, Magic Spells
Treasure and Treason, A Raine Benares World Novel
Ruins and Revenge, A Raine Benares World Novel

ABOUT THE AUTHOR

Lisa Shearin is the *New York Times* bestselling author of the Raine Benares novels, a comedic fantasy adventure series, as well as the SPI Files novels, an urban fantasy series best described as *Men in Black* with supernaturals instead of aliens. Lisa is a voracious collector of fountain pens, teapots, and teacups, both vintage and modern. She lives on a small farm in North Carolina with her husband, four spoiled-rotten retired racing greyhounds, and enough deer and woodland creatures to fill a Disney movie.

Website: lisashearin.com
Facebook: facebook.com/LisaShearinAuthor
Twitter: @LisaShearin

CPSIA information can be obtained
at www.ICGtesting.com
Printed in the USA
LVHW042352251218
601725LV00001B/198/P

9 781732 722606